the **actual
total
truth**

Also by Karen Rivers

Waiting to Dive

Barely Hanging On

Karen Rivers

the actual total truth

Scholastic Canada Ltd.
Toronto New York London Auckland Sydney
Mexico City New Delhi Hong Kong Buenos Aires

Scholastic Canada Ltd.
604 King Street West, Toronto, Ontario M5V 1E1, Canada

Scholastic Inc.
557 Broadway, New York, NY 10012, USA

Scholastic Australia Pty Limited
PO Box 579, Gosford, NSW 2250, Australia

Scholastic New Zealand Limited
Private Bag 94407, Greenmount, Auckland, New Zealand

Scholastic Children's Books
Euston House, 24 Eversholt Street,
London NW1 1DB, UK

Cover photo by Rodrigo Moreno

Library and Archives Canada Cataloguing in Publication

Rivers, Karen, 1970-
The actual total truth / Karen Rivers.

ISBN 978-0-439-93755-9

I. Title.

PS8585.I8778A63 2007   jC813'.54   C2006-906674-4

6 5 4 3 2 1   Printed in Canada   07 08 09 10 11

To my dad, as always, for finding and sharing the island that inspired these books; and to Sonja, for her island encounter.

— K.R.

chapter 1

Treasure is lying on my totally empty belly, purring. At least I think he's purring. Maybe it's my stomach grumbling because I'm starving, but I can't be bothered to go find some food, and also if I eat I'll probably grow taller and that's the last thing I need. Anyway, my mood is much too bad for anything that requires moving. It's Very Bad. I don't even know where to start.

Honestly, I don't know what Treasure has to be so happy about. Granted, he's a cat and doesn't know any better, but I feel like he should be able to pick up on my Horrible, Worst Ever Mood and have the good grace to not be so cheerful near me. Or *on* me. How dare he?

I push him off me, which is no small task because he's grown so much in the last three months it's like he's on his way to becoming the Biggest Cat Ever. He leaves a patch of orange fur on my black T-shirt that is impossible to brush off. I don't know how he does it, but his orange hairs weave into all my clothes like they have little needles on the end and tiny little people sewing them into the fabric. I swear I must stink like a cat at all times. But I love Treasure, even though he is the hairiest, the soon-to-be-biggest and the most orange cat in the world. I found him last February on my island when we were looking for gold. I shouldn't call it *my* island because it isn't *mine,* but my parents have a cabin there, so it's sort of mine. I mean, I'm eleven. It's not like anything is really mine. Except Treasure. And Blue, my dog.

I found three kittens on my island that day (I thought they were the ghost of a crazy old man, but never mind that) and my best friends Sam and Montana kept the other two. They named theirs Grace and Ghost. Both Grace and Ghost are grey, so I'm sure you'll agree that I got the best one, because mine is the most different and everyone knows that being different is better than being the same, unless you are so different that it's just peculiar. It is only fair that I got to choose my kitten first because they were found on my birthday. (I have a third best friend, Felicia, who was there, but she's allergic to cats and so she didn't get one at all.) You have to feel sorry for Felicia for not getting a cat, but at the same time, there were only three cats and four best friends so it really worked out for the best. You do the math, you'll see what I mean.

Not that I'm an expert in math or anything. Math. Huh. Don't get me started.

This ugly carpet is now itching my stomach, but I'm not going to move. It is specifically *not* the chocolate brown carpeting that I picked out for my new bedroom. This is because this is my *old* bedroom, which soon will be converted into a nursery for the New Baby. I go cross-eyed staring at the carpet. If you go cross-eyed and stare at patterns of dots, sometimes you can see other stuff, like sailboats or creepy faces, but that is not the case here.

I swear to you, everything in this house revolves around the New Baby. The New Baby is really going to have it made when he/she shows up. I suppose I'll just sleep in the garage or in the living room or on the front lawn when he/she comes and needs this room. Who knows? It's not like anyone cares. Believe me, when there is a New Baby coming, nothing else matters, including strange-looking not-quite-adolescent girls with troubles of their own.

Big troubles.

To make a long story short, my new, perfect, chosen-by-me bedroom was given to our temporary nanny, Jenny, because of the New Baby. Or rather because my mum was too tired to look after us properly. "Us" being, of course, me (Carly) and my little step-sister Marly (I know it rhymes, okay? Lame. Believe me, this is one of the banes of my existence.) And my littler step-brother Shane. Like we were too much work just because Mum's got a stomach the size of a Volkswagen Beetle (my favourite car, in case you were wondering) and sleeps for fifty hours a day, in between throwing up and complaining. Not that she shouldn't complain. Throwing up is the most disgusting thing in the world. What's grosser? Nothing, that's what.

Why anyone would want to be pregnant is a complete mystery to me, but I guess because I'm my mum's and the other two kids belong to my step-dad, my parents wanted to have one together. You know, like hers, his and *theirs*. What. And *ever*. When they show those *Don't Get Pregnant as a Teenager* movies at school, they should include footage of my mum being sick for the ten-thousandth time and then show the veins on her legs. Seriously. You have no idea. Anyone in their right mind would reconsider having a baby if they got a gander at those lumpy strings, let me tell you.

In the backyard, I can hear the dogs barking, which means that any second now Dad is going to shout at me and make me take them for a walk because my mum is resting and Can't Be Disturbed. (He's not my Real Dad. He died. He's my step-dad, who I call Dad because, let's face it, calling someone Step-Dad would be really odd.)

It's only the end of June and the baby's not coming out until July. I guess as it gets ready to hatch, Mum's even sleepier than ever, which is pretty funny. I think she's awake for five minutes a day. Don't tell her, but I sort of miss her. I mean I miss the *old* her, that used to go out jogging and take me to diving and watch my gymnastics practices. I'll kind of be glad when the New Baby is finally here, not because I *care*, but because I'm tired of my mum being Too Tired to do the junk that's important to me, even though it probably isn't very important at all. You know what I mean. For example, she's Too Tired to take me to diving practice or to pick me up so I have to beg rides from friends and I feel like, well, a beggar. Like my diving isn't important to Mum anymore now that there is a New Baby on the way. It's New Baby this, New Baby that around here at all times. Seriously.

Not that I'm bitter.

Okay, so I am.

Bitter-Ella, my friend Montana calls me. Montana is so nice it's sometimes just a tiny bit repulsive. Also, she has beautiful hair, which is black and shiny. She says that she's jealous that I'm going to have a baby to play with, but she doesn't know what it's really like. Trust me. They aren't all cuteness and fun. They cry and barf and need their diapers changed and burp like mad all over you. It's not like they come out and start running around the room playing tag and gooing and gahing in an adorable way or anything. They just lie there, wrinkled and sobbing! My mum made me go to this class at the community centre about dealing with new babies. (Boring.) (And also grosser than I would have thought.) Now that I've taken it, I'm pretty much an expert, and I can tell you that babies are no walk in the park.

Anyway, wait until I win my Olympic gold medal. Just wait for *that.* That will show everyone, especially Mum. She'll be sorry that she was soooo tired and couldn't help me. She'll probably feel pretty bad when I say, "I'd like to thank all my friends' mums for *not* being Too Tired to give me a ride home from diving practice." Not that I *want* her to feel bad. I mean, I am happy about this baby in my own way. (I overheard Dad saying that to Mum the other day. "I'm sure Carly is happy *in her own way.*" I like that, because it's true.) Which is to say, I'm not really very happy but I'll get used to it. I got used to having Marly and Shane around, didn't I? I'm not totally mean to them anymore.

I hope.

Not being mean is very, very, very important to me. No one wants to be the mean kid. I want to be the nice kid that everyone likes, like Montana. And also, I want to be famous. Then I want everyone to reminisce about me as a kid and for them to say, "Oh, Carly, she was soooooo nice! If anyone deserves this, she does!" Frankly, I don't think mean people get to be famous as often as nice people. Think about it. Pretend it's the Olympics, okay? Are you going to clap for a mean person or a nice person?

I pull a thread on my ugly old bedspread and half an ugly old flower unravels. Great. I wind the thread around my finger really tightly just to watch the end of my finger turn purple. Once, in science class, we had to do an experiment with blood so we had to cut off the circulation to our fingertips like that. And then we pronged the end of our fingers with sterilized pins so that blood squirted out. We did tests to see what kind of blood we had. Mine is A-positive, which looks like A+ when you write it down.

So, you see, even my blood gets better marks than I do, which is part of the reason why I'm in a No Good, Horrible, Blah Mood. I just found out that my teacher, Mrs. Witless, has called my dad at work and told him that she thinks that I would "benefit" from taking some stupid math class in summer school. Which means a whole bunch of things, like that I'm dumb and a failure and maybe she'll make me repeat Grade Five if I don't take it. I'm so much stupider than everyone else all of a sudden, I can't figure out why. I mean, I shouldn't be dumb. I read a lot. Really, I do. Mum always said that reading makes you smart, so I've read almost all of her old books that she had when she was a girl, and ancient books she kept from her own mum when *she* was a girl. I love them. I love the way they talk in some of those really old books. Oh, man. They say things like "ought" and "shan't." I wish people still talked like that.

Anyway, if I fail Grade Five, my life will be over, I swear. Think about it. I'm already *way* taller than everyone in the class. Freakishly, horribly, dreadfully tall. So if I had to do Grade Five again next year, I'd be like a giant in a land of dwarves. Seriously. It would be way too traumatizing for everyone. I *shan't* do it. So there.

If I have to take this dumb math class then I guess I have to do it. Honestly, I'm very disappointed and shocked and mad. It's going to get in the way of my Summer Holiday, which everyone knows is the whole *point* of life. I mean, everyone else will be outside and having fun and taking tennis lessons and swimming and going to the beach, and I'll be stuck in a stuffy classroom being reminded that I'm too dumb to have the summer off. Frankly, it makes me very angry. I don't know what I'm angry at *specifically,* so don't ask. Maybe I'm angry at God for making me less good at math than other people. Or at Montana for being so smart and getting straight *As* and saying that she'd be happy to help me with my math. (I mean, that was *nice* of her. See how she's really nice? She would get lots of applause at the Olympics, let me tell you.) But she obviously doesn't know how dumb it makes me feel to have her offer to help me. I *hate* it.

My stomach aches when I start thinking about the Olympics and how everyone in the world would love her and maybe they wouldn't like me as much, but they would refer to me as "that nice Montana's friend." My mum says I worry too much about stuff that is never going to happen, but she doesn't know. How can she predict? Things are always happening. There, a wasp just flew into my window. *Thud.* That was something happening. I should add that I'm allergic to wasp stings, so if it got in I'd have to run around like a monkey with ants in my pants to avoid getting stung.

Anyway, like I mentioned, I'm suddenly very tall. And when I say suddenly, I mean *suddenly.* Like overnight, only that can't be true, but it feels true. All I know is that one day, magically, my pants were all too short (which, believe me, looks dumber than dumb) and I kept falling off the balance beam in gymnastics and hitting my head on stuff. Sometimes I wake up at night crying because my legs ache so much. The doctor said that it is just a Growth Spurt. Then he laughed, like it was the funniest thing in the world. Well,

I'm telling you that being five foot seven in Grade Five is not funny and it makes gymnastics very difficult, not to mention everything else, like trying to not look like the Tallest Person in the World. I used to be very very good at gymnastics. Not as good as I was at diving, but excellent all the same. You know how you can tell you're good at something? When you're doing it and it just feels right. I always knew exactly where my arms and legs and chin and feet were, exactly, even in the air. I can't really explain. But now, suddenly, my body is kooky. I've lost sight of myself. I know it sounds crazy. But my feet are further away than they should be and everything is knocked off balance by my gross, ugly height. Being tall is highly overrated, let me tell you.

In fact, to tell you the truth, I quit gymnastics last week after I fell off the balance beam and hit my head on the edge of the crash pad and scratched my chin on some stupid Velcro that was there for no reason and not even where I expected my chin to land.

I was wounded!

The coach made me get up and do it again. She's very hostile. So I told her I was through — really and truly done with it — and I stomped off. It was just too much. I haven't actually told anyone in my family yet that I've quit, but I'm going to. I mean, I've already decided. I don't even care.

The only thing I really like about gymnastics is the chalk that you get to put on your hands to stop yourself from falling off the bar and stuff, and watching other people flip around. It looks neat. It kind of hurts though. It bruises your hips.

I also liked the way my body felt at home in the gym, but now it doesn't. It feels like someone else's body. I hate it. I don't know what to do about it. I need to shrink. I really, really do. I mean, why isn't there a pill?

What I'm really scared of is that if my freakish height has messed up my gymnastics, maybe it will mess up my diving, too. It hasn't *yet*, but maybe it's just a matter of time. Huh! And that's like my all-time number-one dream — to dive at the Olympics.

To make matters worse (like they could be worse), I didn't get any fatter — just taller — so now I'm all stretched out and gangly. My mum says it's cute and that I look like a model, which just goes to show you that my mum is delusional (which means crazy, in case you don't know). The truth is that I look like Skeletor from the He-Man cartoons that you see on those old rerun channels. I never used to be allowed to watch TV, but now my dad lets me because it "keeps me out of trouble." In other words, it keeps me away from my mum. Well, it's a good thing I've seen the show because now I know who the dumb boys in my class are referring to when they yell, "Hey, Skeletor, how's the weather up there?"

Mrs. Witless says it's just because they're jealous and *short,* but Mrs. Witless is not exactly a fountain of sparkling knowledge.

My best friends (Sam, Felicia and Montana, of course) say that I look fine and that I'm normal and that they wish they were tall, too. But they are just lying to make me feel better, which is what best friends are required to do. Especially tiny, properly sized best friends with shiny hair and nice personalities and good grades in Math. All of them. And they are all nice, although I think Sam is more like me, in that sometimes she isn't always thinking the nicest things. Felicia and Montana are freakishly nice. Felicia is shy, too, but Sam is totally not. It's funny that we're all friends. We all look so different and we act totally differently most of the time. Montana is very smart and confident and pretty *and* nice and my most seriously best friend. Felicia is Sam's most seriously best friend even though she's not very athletic the way Sam is. Sam is gangbusters. She's so cool. She says whatever she thinks. Sometimes she gets in trouble at diving though — she talks a leeetle too much, if you know what I mean.

Anyway. That pretty much sums it up, then. I guess you can see why I might not be capital-*h*

Happy. I'm a dumb, giant string bean with bad balance and a step-sister with a rhyming name who right now is banging on my door, shouting, "Carly! Carly! Come and play tea party!" If only a tea party involved actual food, I'd probably jump at the chance. A foodless tea party with funny-tasting warm water in tiny china cups is approximately the last thing in the world I want to participate in, but I do it anyway, because she's one of the last people in the world who doesn't think of me as a big huge giant dumb freak (except my BFFs, of course). Probably it's only because she's so dumb herself, but I try not to think like that. Really, I'm *trying* to be a nicer person. So I smile at her and I say, "Coming, Mealy," which is sort of my little cute nickname for her. She doesn't mind it. She never complains.

She grabs onto my hand and drags me down the hall to her tiny bedroom, which is, well, not that much bigger than a storage closet. This is because it used to be the walk-in closet in my parents' room, but Dad whacked away at the walls with a hammer for a while and turned it into a tiny room. I'm kind of jealous because I like tiny rooms. When I was smaller, I used to like to sit in my bedroom closet at our old house and read those funny old English books, like *The Famous Five* and *The Secret Seven.* If you haven't read them, you should. Really, they were way better than, like, Bobbsey

Twins and Sweet Valley whatever.

Her room is cute now. There is pretty cool stuff painted on the walls. On one wall, there is a giant dolphin jumping out of the water and leaving a rainbow. I *love* that dolphin. Also, it must be nice to have your very own bedroom that's not just temporarily yours while you're waiting for your real bedroom to be freed up.

I swallow hard so that I don't start getting mad again. I look for a light, which is an old trick of mine to stop my anger from coming out — if I squint at it long enough, I don't get so mad. It seems to me that I have a lot to be mad about, though. But I make myself smile instead. When you make yourself smile and you're not really happy, it feels weird. I can feel air on my teeth. My cheeks sort of hurt.

When Marly walks, she bobs up and down and her bright red curls bounce around her head like springs. I feel a bit sorry for her. Because even though I didn't get my New Bedroom, my bedroom now is at least large enough to move around in. And even though I didn't get good hair, at least no one calls me Carrot Top, or worse, which I'm sure will plague her throughout her entire school life. Kids are mean sometimes. You have no idea.

We are just sitting down when I hear Dad shouting something from downstairs, so I yell back, "WHAT!" And he yells something else that I can't hear, and the dogs — Roo and Blue — start barking, and Shane, who is three, starts crying. I swear, this is the noisiest house in the world. In the last two months, two of our neighbours have moved away. Coincidence? You decide.

Not that I blame Roo or Blue. Roo is my old dog. She's huge and leaves hair everywhere "with extreme diligence" — that's what Mum says. She thinks Roo makes sure she never lies down in the same place twice just to maximize her hair coverage. Blue's hair doesn't come out. It's blackish-brown and curly. Blue is still practically a puppy. He's very cute. I can hear Dad shouting some more so I put down my tiny teacup of warm water and go to the top of the stairs so I can actually hear what he's hollering. He's shouting, "It's time! We have to go, NOW!" At first I don't know what he means. I'm hoping he means, "IT'S TIME FOR LUNCH." But I know he doesn't, because he never sounds so excited about lunch. Although *I* would be. (It takes a lot of food to grow this much, believe me.) But I look at his face, and I feel my heart drop to the bottom of my shoes and I hug Marly, who starts crying because she sees my mum at the front door and there is a big gross puddle under her, like she's just peed her pants, and her face is as white as a sheet, and all I can think of to do is whisper, "Bye, Mum," and then they are gone.

She's having the baby. It's hatching!

I hear the car squeal a bit at the bottom of the driveway, like they are driving in such a huge hurry they don't even have time to put on the brakes at the bottom of the hill.

I must say, it all makes my heart speed up quite a bit. It's pounding in my chest like it's going to come right out. I wouldn't be surprised if it leapt away and bounced down the stairs like one of those really hard rubber balls that bounce so high they sometimes hit the ceiling, even when you didn't mean them to. Although sometimes it's fun to do that — throw the ball at the ground so hard that it ricochets off the wall and the ceiling and off everything in the room. Unless it breaks something, such as a vase that someone got as a wedding gift. Not that this has ever happened to me.

"I'm scared," says Marly.

"Don't be scared," I tell her. "It just means that the baby in mummy's tummy is going to come out! We should go downstairs and make a *Welcome Home, Baby* sign." I mean, I am just trying to think of things to distract Marly so she doesn't freak out, but the truth is that I am a bit scared myself. I don't really know all of it, but I know it's been a "difficult" pregnancy, whatever that means, and it's all, well, scary. What if the baby comes out wrong? I mean, I don't know what could go wrong, but I could imagine an awful lot of things if I try. Which I try not to do. I mean, it's not like worrying about it is going to help or anything. Besides, people have perfectly normal babies all the time. Look around you! Everyone was once a baby. Everyone once came out. Somehow.

Just then, Jenny — who is our nanny even though I think I'm too old to have a nanny — emerges from downstairs. (Mum tells me to think of her more as a "mother's helper," which is even worse than "nanny" if you ask me.)

"Hey, I have an idea!" she says. "Let's make some *Welcome Home* signs for your mum and the new baby while we're waiting to hear from them!"

Jenny is very nice and has a handsome boyfriend. I like her. And so I don't tell her that that was already my idea. It doesn't matter, I guess, that I thought of it first. All that matters is that Shane and Marly have something to do so they don't get scared and start wondering exactly how it is that a baby comes out. Believe me, I've thought about it, and all the exit points seem pretty small, if you know what I mean. It can't be anything good.

We pull out our paper and markers and get to work. I stick my tongue between my teeth and concentrate really hard on filling in the *W* that I made, with stars and dots and flowers. It's a big *W*. To tell you the truth, it may be disproportionately big for the sign, but it doesn't matter. I'm just going to make it the most beautiful *W* in the world. Jenny puts some music on and starts singing and dancing with Shane. Marly starts colouring big scribbles in some of the other letters. Outside, it starts to rain really really hard and the sound of the rain hammering on the windows almost drowns out the sound of my heart hammering in my chest.

My hands are turning purple from the ink and Marly is getting bored and starting to do this really annoying whining thing she does where she says, "I'm not whining," in this really whiny voice.

Whoa.

I may not be good at math, but I've already figured out that by the time the baby that mum is having right now is five, I'll be sixteen. I mean, I'll practically be old enough to move out! Which means that virtually the entire time that I'm a kid, I'll be subject to some kind of whiny siblings. Great. To make myself feel better, I go into the kitchen to sneak some cookies and to call Montana. Montana, on top of being the best person in the world and my BFF, has the best phone number. It's almost all 3's, which is my favourite number. I love it when I call her and her mum answers in her funny accent. Montana and her family are from the Philippines. I wish I was from the Philippines. It sounds interesting and exotic, which I'm not. To be honest, sometimes I feel a little green when I think about Montana. My mum says that "green" is the colour that you get when you're jealous. And Montana makes me green. But she's so great, I can't hate her. Last summer, she was in the most terrible, awful, horrible diving-off-the-rocks accident at my summer cabin and she *broke her back*. It was the worst thing in the world you can imagine. Please don't make me talk about it. I will be friends with her forever, no matter what, because it's my fault that she had to quit diving and now has really superior posture because she has a steel rod in her spine. I have bad posture. Big surprise there, huh?

On my way into the kitchen, I stop at the mirror in the hallway to inspect my skin for pimples. I don't have any yet, but I probably will one day. It's not that I want them, I just want to be constantly vigilant in case they appear. I've already started using this blue stuff on my face that stings like the dickens but apparently stops you from getting zits. It makes my face go bright red, but that's okay. It's got to be good for you.

There is nothing worse than zits. There is this odd-looking kid, Smith, in my class at school who is more, um, mature than the other kids and he has zits. Like he didn't already have terrible luck, what with the weird colouring and white hair. He's funny, though. Sometimes he's nice, which is saying a lot about a boy in Grade Five. Don't even get me started about Tim the Nose Blower who did guess what on the valentine I made for him. Huh. Revolting pig.

I sit down at the table and start chomping hard on a cookie. It's not very good, but I'm so hungry that I don't care. I break half of it off for Blue, who followed me in. Blue stinks, because of the rain. His thick curly hair has a tendency to stink more often than not, frankly. I throw the cookie into the corner of the room just to get him as far away from my nose as possible and I dial Montana's number, which is busy. Haven't they heard of call waiting?

I think about whether to call Sam or Felicia, seeing as they are also my best friends, but not as much as Montana is, and I decide not to. I really *like* them, but sometimes I run out of things to say on the phone and I feel dumb calling for no reason, like I always have to be calling them to invite them over or something. I'm just sitting there thinking about that when the phone rings and nearly scares me to death. I'm so startled that I almost don't answer it, and then I'm glad that I do because it's Montana, and she was trying to call me the whole time.

"My mum went to the hospital!" I tell her, and she's all excited. She knows it's really important to me that my new sister/brother has a cool name, i.e. one that doesn't rhyme with mine, and so she says, "Did they pick a name yet?"

And I say, "No, not yet, they wanted to wait until it was born just to make sure everything is okay." Then for some reason I just burst into tears, which was really an odd thing to do and I'm glad I did it in front of Montana and not someone else who might not understand.

She just says, "It's going to be fine, Carly."

And I say, "I know it is, I'm just, it's just, I don't know. It's just weird."

The call waiting beeps. "I have to go," I tell her. I'm a little relieved, if you must know. It's hard to recover from randomly crying like a baby for no particular reason. It's my dad.

"Well?" I say. "Tell me."

"There's nothing to tell yet," he says. He sounds tired already, like he's been up all night even though he's only been gone for half an hour. "It might be a while."

"I see," I say, even though I don't.

"So I just wanted to call and tell you everything is fine and not to worry."

"Okay," I say, and hang up. I mean, really, that was a bit pointless — why call if you don't have any news? I take the pad and paper which are always beside the telephone and start writing down lists of names that I like. I like names with Zs in them. I like the name Zoë and the name Maizy. Even though Dad says that *maize* is like a

French word for corn, so that would really mean "corny." Okay, so maybe I don't like it that much. But I like Zoë for a girl. For a boy, I keep changing my mind. I told my mum that I liked the name Zane, but that's just because it rhymes with Shane and I wanted her to see how weird and stupid it was to have rhyming names.

Maybe I like the name Jacob. Or Nicholas. Or Max. It's super-hard to think of a boy's name and I know I have to work on it because my mum said that I got a vote in the decision. She actually said that I could name the baby, but then she sort of took that back because she has veto power, which essentially means that whatever I pick she can say no to and then just pick something else. Whatever.

I can hear the kids squealing in the other room, which makes me want to go for a walk, so I grab that stinker Blue and put a leash on him and yell at Jenny, "I'm going for a walk!" I leave Roo behind because she is so old that walking is hard for her. There is something wrong with her hips. I always feel bad walking Blue without Roo.

Walking in the rain is weird, because you get soaked, but also because rain prongs into your eyes and it stings a little. For good measure, I do a bit more crying. I'm not sad, but I have a bit of anxiety inside me and crying is good for that, or so my mum says. And besides, crying in the rain doesn't count because no one can see it.

We walk for quite a long time. Blue is not very good at walking on a leash and he keeps crossing in front of me and nearly tripping me and killing me on the sidewalk, which would be a fine kettle of fish. We kind of accidentally dropped out of obedience school early on. There was another dog there that scared the dickens out of me, if you must know. Besides, Blue is very well-behaved if you don't count the part where he can't walk on a leash. I tug on it and growl, "Heeeeeeeel." Like he'll automatically know what "heel" means. It's just that I have enough problems without a sprained ankle or a broken leg.

It's pretty cold and does not feel like the end of June. Next week is the last week of school, and that means that we just go to school and sit around and don't really do anything. One day we're going to the beach and another day we're going to the museum. They're very big on the museum around here and drag us down there at least once or twice a year. It's a neat museum, I must admit. There's lots of cool stuff there. But it's hardly school or important. They should spend more time teaching us dumb math so we don't have to take summer school and less time dragging us around to places we've been a billion and one times and could go to on our own during our summer holidays.

So it's basically summer holidays now and it feels like October. Seriously. It's raining like a bazillion drops per minute and I'm soaked through to the skin. I keep walking because even though I'm wet and cold, at least it's quiet except for the sound of cars occasionally going by and splooshing me with water and the sound of Blue's panting. He's a little bit fat. This is a serious workout for him. I'm in very good shape so it's no skin off my nose. I start to run a bit to make him work. Exercise is very important, as I'm sure you know. It's much quieter out here than being at home waiting for the phone to ring and listening to whining and crying kids.

Sometimes I think I'll probably never have kids when I grow up. I'll live alone in a beautiful apartment and no one will be noisy and bug me. Or maybe I'll have some kids and then get divorced so I only have to deal with them part of the time. That's what it's like for Marly and Shane's mum. She lives in an apartment and the kids go to her place on the weekends now, but not all the time. Every other week, mostly, except when we have them. It must be weird but also nice and peaceful.

I pass by the school, which is totally empty because it's Sunday. It looks different when it's empty — hollow and scary. I decide to play some hopscotch by myself. I mean, why not? Sure, it's for little kids, but it's not like anyone can see me. Besides, it's fun.

Huh.

Hopscotch, like most things, is significantly less fun when you are alone, is what I find out. For one thing, it's not hard to win. My mum says I'm too competitive, but I can't help it, I like to win things. When there is no one to play against, it's just lame. I should have called Sam or Felicia to see if they wanted to come with me for the walk but they might have laughed at me for hopscotching any-way. Felicia lives very close to the school. I squint through the rain to try to see her house when all of a sudden a rolling gallop of thunder startles me half to death. Blue practically jumps into my arms. Then there is a great big crack, and a giant terrifying snap of lightning strikes down so close to me I swear I can hear a tree sizzle.

Now I'm scared, I don't mind admitting. I start to run for real, which is hard because I keep trip-ping over the leash and Blue is dragging his heels. Finally, I just let Blue go and figure that he'll fol-low me. What if I get hit by lightning? Seriously, that is something that would happen to me. That's the kind of luck that I have. By the time I'm in sight of my house, I'm shivering and sweating from running and also completely out of breath. Poor Blue is dragging his leash behind him. He looks like a drowned rat, as my dad would say, not that I'm sure he's ever actually seen a drowned rat or anything. I know I haven't. And how would a drowned rat look any different from a regular wet rat, except for being dead?

I push the front door open and Jenny is standing there with her coat on and the kids are already in the car. *"There* you are!" she says, "You've been ages! Your mum has had the baby and we're on our way to see it! Get in the car, right away!"

So before I even have time to ask what the baby is or if it's okay or anything, I'm whipped into the car and dripping all over the seat as we whiz through the storm towards the hospital on the other side of town.

chapter 2

It's a boy!

Jenny tells me as we drive to the hospital. I
don't know how to feel about this. I keep saying,
"It's a boy! It's a boy!" In a way, I wanted it to be a
boy. But the girl stuff you can buy for babies is so
cute, I also wanted it to be a girl.

"It's a boy!" I say again.

"It's a boy!" says Marly. Then she says it over
and over and I realize how annoying it is, so I stop
doing it.

As soon as we get to the hospital, I start to feel
all weird and light-headed, like I can't breathe,
never mind the fact that I'm wet and cold. The
almost last time I was here was when I was visiting Montana after she broke her back. (The really
last time was when we got to see an ultrasound of
the baby when Mum was pregnant. Ultrasounds,
in case you don't know, let you look at the baby
while it's inside. It pretty much looks like a baby

that doesn't do anything.) I guess Mum's not pregnant anymore, which is funny when you think about it. She's been pregnant for so long (it seems like forever, but it's really only nine long months, which is most of a year) and suddenly she's just . . . not.

I'm nervous to see her, so I dig my nails into the palm of my hand to stop myself from feeling scared. Is her belly going to have flattened out again or will it be just a big empty deflated ball? What happens to all that skin? Is the baby going to be as huge as her belly? Because, seriously, her belly was ginormous. It looked big enough for me to crawl into and curl up in.

I kind of snort with laughter thinking about a baby being born at five foot seven inches tall, and then I realize that we're already on the right floor. Everyone else is half-running down the hall, Jenny holding onto Shane and Marly racing after them. Huh. I almost let the doors close to see if they notice that I'm missing. But then I get excited again and I hurry to catch up and forget about how nervous I am. All the while I'm thinking of boys' names that I like, or I'm *trying* to think of boys' names that I like, because all of a sudden now that there's a real live baby boy to name, all the names that I can think of sound incredibly lame and horrible, like the names of kids that get stuffed into lockers because they are so strange.

Like Houston, for example. Or Henry.

We burst into Mum's room, just in time to see her covering up her giant naked breast, which was borderline frightening. I mean, I know one day that I'll have boobs, too, but I hope they aren't larger than a pumpkin, you know what I mean? Seriously. Hers are so big you could store things in there. Anyway, I don't think too much about that because there next to her is my new brother. Well, half-brother. I practically fall over my feet stopping so suddenly, almost next to him. He's just lying there, breathing. I don't know what I expected. His face is very red and wrinkly. He looks like a small hairless monkey.

I must say, he doesn't look anything like me. Or Mum. Or Dad. Or anyone else for that matter. He's very squished looking. And so tiny, like if you picked him up, he'd totally break. I kind of hold my breath and Mum says, "Aren't you going to pick him up, Carly?" So, of course, I have to pick him up like it's the most natural thing in the world, which it isn't. Dad has to show me.

"Watch his neck!" he keeps saying.

For Pete's sake, I'm not going to break the baby's neck, although it is significantly wobblier than I would have thought, even bound up in all those blankets. For a second I feel sick, like Dad was reminding me about how Montana broke her back when she was visiting me, so it was sort of my fault, like I'm a back-breaker or something. I make myself stare at the light for a second, just to not get mad or super-defensive. Then I stare at my brother. He's so small! He weighs just about nothing.

"Aw," I say. Even though I'm not sure that I feel it. Is he cute? I really can't tell. He's very scrunched up and a bit purple. I'm terrified that I'm going to drop him and then he'll break and everyone will hate me. I hold my breath.

Under this ugly hat he's wearing, he has a patch of dark, fuzzy hair. Naturally, as soon as I start to feel okay holding him, he wakes up and opens his eyes, which are blue (apparently all new babies' eyes are blue), and starts screaming to beat the band. For such a tiny thing, he sure has good pipes. I quickly give him to Mum and he immediately stops crying, which makes me feel pretty useless, to tell you the truth. Like he's just been born and already my brother doesn't like me. He probably senses that I'm terrible at math and knows to keep a good distance.

Dad helps Marly to sit in the chair and he takes the baby and balances him on Marly's lap. She's so excited, she's practically shaking. I think that she thinks it's a doll. I hope *she* doesn't drop him. Why isn't Dad going on and on and on to her about his neck? In any event, he doesn't cry for her. Hmm. Whatever. It's not like I take it personally.

"We're going to call him Nicholas Zane," says my mum.

"Oooh," says Jenny, "that's just beautiful."

I just blink, because — Hello? — that was supposed to be *my* choice. My mum looks so tired though, and there is makeup smeared under her eyes as well as all this other stuff which is apparently bruising that she got from pushing so hard to get the baby out. (Don't think about this one too much. I know I don't want to.) I don't want to get her all upset. Maybe she just forgot that she was going to ask me for help with the name. Maybe she didn't know it was important. She looks at me and says, "Zane was Carly's favourite name when we asked her. That's why we chose it." Which makes me feel bad, because I did once suggest Zane, but that's only because it rhymed with Shane and I was being a bit mean-ish in suggesting another rhyming name like Marly/Carly. Duh. Still, it's nice that she remembered.

I sit down in the other chair and start kicking my feet. Jenny is ogling the baby and Mum looks half-asleep. I sneak another peek at Nicholas Zane. He still looks the same. I feel like I don't know what to do or say.

"It's raining," I say.

"I can see that," says Mum. "You look wet!"

"I went for a walk."

"Great," she says. She can't take her eyes off

the baby. I feel like ducking down to get into her line of vision, but somehow it seems like that would be rude. I go cross-eyed instead.

"Hey, Carly," says my dad. "Why don't you and I go downstairs and get a piece of pie?"

I once told him that getting a piece of pie in the hospital cafeteria was something that sounded really good to me, and it was really great of him to remember. I pretend to think about it and then I say, "Sure." I don't want to look too excited, because seriously, it's a piece of pie, not a trip to Disneyland or a new car.

"Go," says Mum. "Marly and Shane and Jenny can stay with me and the baby." The baby has gone back to sleep again in this aquarium sort of thing and looks really peaceful, in his weird, wrinkled up, red sort of way. I pat him on his really soft cheek super gently as we walk by, but he doesn't wake up.

In the cafeteria, Dad orders a cup of coffee and I get a piece of apple pie and a cola. I don't usually drink cola and, frankly, I don't much like it, but it seems like the right thing to do at the time. I should have got something hot because I'm seriously cold and wet and my clothes are all sticking to me. I sneeze three times in a row without really sneezing.

"Let the sneeze out!" Dad says. "You'll burst your brain!" Which makes me giggle. I always sneeze in a particular way so as not to let anything out. It does feel a little hollow in my head. Maybe it is blowing up my brain. I sneeze again and I try to let it out, but I can't.

When I drink cola, the bubbles get in my nose and I always have to sneeze at the start of every drink. It's like it takes my body a minute to get used to the bubbly sugar-ness.

"I hope you're not getting a cold," Dad says.

"I'm fine," I explain. "It's the cola." I take a bite of my apple pie, which looks a little sad and saggy. To be perfectly frank, it isn't very good, but the cafeteria is neat. There are rows and rows of Jell-O, which is hilarious because they serve it with every meal when you're a patient here, or they did when Montana was here, anyway. The last thing you'd want if you broke out of your room and got into the hospital cafeteria would be more Jell-O. Who orders it? Just when I was thinking that, I see a doctor buying a bowl of green Jell-O. GREEN! For real. I didn't know anyone liked green. What's it supposed to be, anyway? Lime? I know she's a doctor because she's in a white coat and has a stethoscope around her neck. She looks really happy about her lime (or whatever) Jell-O. I wonder if she actually loves it and feels jealous whenever she sees it on her patients' trays and has to sneak down here to satisfy her cravings. Maybe her unusual passion for it made her want to be a doctor in the first place, knowing that hospitals are filled to overflowing with the stuff.

I don't want to be a doctor, which is probably a good thing as I'm not very bright. Montana does, though. She's so smart, I'm sure she'll be a huge success.

Which gets me to thinking how I'm not smart anymore. I used to be, but it stopped. I don't know where it went, all that smartness. I must have sneezed it gone.

I sigh vigorously and nearly choke on some pie pastry, which is too gluey for words. Yuck. Talk about disappointing. I pretend I'm not shivering by sitting on my hands.

"So Carly," says Dad, "A new brother, huh!"

"Right!" I say. "Nice!" I mean, I'm not sure what else to say. "He's cute!"

"He sure is," says Dad, with a weird dreamy look in his eyes.

"You bet," I say.

"Nicholas Zane," he says.

"Uh huh," I say. I pour some sugar on the table and draw a pattern in it. This conversation is a bit dull, to tell you the honest to Pete truth. "Nice baby," I say.

"Right," he says, suddenly snapping back to life. "Anyway, Carly," he goes on, "I was wanting to ask you something."

"What?" I say. I'm a bit distracted by looking around to see what other people are eating. A lot of people are eating something that looks like spaghetti, but with shorter noodles. It must be the special of the day, which is listed on the board as Lasagna Casserole. I nibble on the crust of my pie by putting my face down near my plate so I don't have to disturb my hand/arm arrangement. It tastes like wet sand. Yum. Or not.

"Well, this weekend is the lowest tide of the year," he says. "I know this is going to sound awful. It sounds awful to me. I can't believe I'm going to do it, to tell you the truth. But your mother insists. Her mother and sister are coming for the weekend to help her. Oh . . . I don't know." His voice trails off.

"Uh huh," I say. "Right." Even though I don't really know what he's talking about, I'm trying to make a supportive sound. He looks like he might cry. Since when is the tide a crying issue? We usually only talk about the tide when we talk about going to the cabin, which like I mentioned is on this really cool little island. You can only get there by boat. But we haven't even opened the cabin up yet this year because of Mum and the New Baby coming and all that. And besides, there is still a week of school left.

"So I was thinking — well, your mother was saying — that I should go up to the cabin this weekend and get the mooring up," he says. "I know the timing isn't good, what with the baby coming a bit early and all, but it's the only weekend of the year to get the mooring block sunk fairly easily."

I should tell you that there is a drama of epic proportions every year that involves sinking a giant block of concrete into the ocean in front of where the cabin is and attaching this floating buoy thing to a chain and a rope. The buoy floats and then when we visit, we attach our boat to it. It seems like an awful lot of trouble, if you ask me, but Dad doesn't like to use the anchor because he says it's too risky.

Anyway, I stare at him. I'm shocked. I really am. All through the pregnancy, Mum had a big red fit if he went anywhere out of town for work or whatever. And now she's chasing him out of the house? When the baby is brand new?

Not only that, Grandma's coming?

"Your mother says it's okay!" he adds, like he's in trouble, which is pretty funny. "She wants me to do it. It's the tide! It's the only weekend . . . " He starts rambling on and on, a tiny bit like a crazy person. I can tell he's totally eaten up about this.

But to be honest, I can feel myself starting to brighten up inside. If he goes up and gets the mooring done, that means the summer is officially really here and Cabin Season begins! Yippee!

The cabin is my most favourite place in the whole world, simply because it's the best place. If you'd been there, you'd know. There is nowhere better. Not even Hawaii. It's all beaches and forests and ocean and deer and raccoons and starfish and huge barnacle-covered rocks and sandstone that goes on for miles. And that's it. There are no roads, except for logging roads because the logging company comes every once in a while and takes down a whole bunch of trees and leaves really big ugly patches of scrub. But other than that, there are no cars or trucks on the island and no phones or anything, unless you bring your own cell phone, which most people do. It doesn't sound great, but that's because I'm not explaining it well. Sometimes if you're lucky, you see killer whales and eagles and porpoises and even ghosts that turn out to be cats. You have to take my word for it. I've had the best times of my life at the cabin, looking for gold with my friends and diving off the rock and going for walks in the woods and catching minnows in the tidal pools on the beach. At least, I did when I was little. I hope I still do. Mum is always saying stuff like, "Sooner or later, you'll rather stay home with your friends than hang out with us." So maybe it's true. But for now, I just really want to go to the cabin.

Blah blah blah, Dad is saying. He's fidgeting with the creamers on the table like crazy.

"Huh?" I say, because I accidentally wasn't listening. Sometimes that happens and I get all caught up in my own head. My pie came with a piece of cheese all wrapped up in its own plastic and I start playing with it to sort of keep him company in his fidgeting. I never understood the love people have for putting cheese on their apple pie. Gross. Seriously.

"I thought you could help and then we'd both be . . . " he explains. "Well," he finishes lamely, "we'll both be out of the way of Grandma and Mum and the baby stuff." He knocks on the table. "Try to stick with me, Carly. I know it's been an exciting day."

"Yeah," I agree. "It has been really exciting. I'm glad it's a boy because now there are two of each, right? So it's, like, balanced. It would be weird for Shane if he was the only boy and everyone else was a girl. Well, except you, of course. Duh."

"Right," he says. "Carly, did you listen to the part where I asked if you wanted to invite your friends to the cabin this weekend? We have to go up anyway and we might as well make it . . . special. You probably want to stay home with the baby, though . . . Maybe we should all stay home and . . . "

"Wait! Of course!" I say, like I'm all excited, too excited for him to change his mind, even though I actually didn't hear that part because I wasn't completely listening. "Yes!" I add, for good measure. I don't know how much help a bunch of eleven-year-old girls are going to be to him, but maybe he just wants the company. Or maybe Mum asked him to take me to get me out of her hair while she plays with the New Baby, who is still New Baby in my head even though now he has his own name, Nicholas Zane. NZ. Like New Zealand, only different.

I wish I had a Z initial. There is something about the letter Z that is cooler than the other letters. Carly Z. Abbott-Fitzgerald. That would sound great.

I changed my name once before. Maybe I can change it again. But what would the Z stand for? It would have to be Zoë, and while I thought I liked that name, I've decided now that I don't.

I look up at the clock. I'm dying to go home and call Sam and Felicia and Montana and ask if they can come up to the cabin for the weekend, but I realize that would make it seem like I wasn't interested in the New Baby, which I am, but I don't think he is going to do much more than cry and sleep right now, and it's not like I haven't just spent time with him. I tap on the table with my fingers.

"Let's go back up," says my dad, "and see how everyone's doing." He seems totally sad, like he thinks he's abandoning his entire family to go sink some stupid mooring, and I can tell that it's one of those "crazy" things that Mum has in her head that she's making him do, even though he'd rather stay home. Mum is very adamant about things. Dad sometimes complains about her "agenda." Whatever that means. But she bosses him around anyway and he always does what she says. I think he's worried she'll be secretly mad if he goes, though. I kind of feel sorry for him. Mum — especially when she was pregnant — was very hard to read. Sometimes she'd say "Do this!" and if you did it, she'd get mad because she didn't mean it.

"Okay," I say. But I'm not really in the spirit of looking at the New Baby anymore — isn't that weird? — because I'm already mentally packing my bag with all the stuff I need to make a really great First Weekend at the Cabin, like some books and towels and bathing suit and sunscreen and candy and snacks, for example.

Back in the room, Marly and Shane are getting restless, if by restless I mean that Shane is crying and Marly is pulling his hair. Shane does not have red hair like Marly — he has this beautiful dark curly hair. He looks like an angel, but you just have to get to know him first. Really, he's a pain. Shane the Pain. He is really cute, but only in pictures, when you can't hear him. When he's crying, he bugs me. I guess that's normal. I mean, I can't make him stop crying and he's so loud. Also, the New Baby, NZ, is crying, but he isn't really crying so much as whimpering. Mum looks like she wants to cry, too. "Please go," she says imploringly, which is only a little rude. I don't mind because I want to go, but to tell us to go? Huh. Besides, does she really mean it?

Poor Dad totally hesitates. "You mean, me?" he says.

"No!" she says. "I meant the kids."

"Oh," he says. He plops himself down on the bed. He looks so tired. I feel a bit bad for him.

"Bye, Mum," I say, and kiss her on the cheek. It's sort of creepy to have her lying in a hospital bed. I want to ask her if I can see her deflated stomach, but under the sheet it still looks pretty inflated, so I don't ask. Her stomach was something she was really self-conscious about, especially when it was growing by about a foot a day. I'd make jokes about it and she'd get mad. So I knew that she was upset.

"Bye, Carly," she says. "Be good. I'll be home tomorrow."

Tomorrow? Wha-huh? They sure don't let you stay for very long. "Okay," I say. "See you." It seems so nutso that she went to the hospital today without a baby and tomorrow she'll be home with a baby. But I don't have too much time to think about it, because tomorrow is also the start of The Last Week of School, which means it is also seriously time for Countdown to Summer.

"Can we stop for ice cream on the way home?" I ask Jenny as we go down the elevator. Elevators make me a tad nervous. Where does the air come from? What if they get stuck? "It's Countdown to Summer."

"It's so cold and rainy," she says dubiously. She kind of looks at me. The elevator lurches, and I grab onto Marly just to have something to hold onto. She kicks me in the shin. Nice.

"It doesn't matter," I tell her. "It's tradition."

"Well, okay," she says. "I guess today is a special occasion."

"Totally," I say. "It's the last Sunday before summer holidays, which means it's the last Sunday before a Monday where I have to get up early to go to school." (I'm purposely not thinking about the fact that with Math for Tortured Losers all summer, I'm going to have to continue to get up early. Pooh.)

"Actually, I meant it was a special day because Nicholas was born," she says.

"Oh!" I say. It takes me a minute to think of who Nicholas *is*, to tell you the truth. I already think of him as NZ in my mind, which makes me think of New Zealand, which makes me think of sheep. I did a report on New Zealand at school this year and there are more sheep there than people.

"Obviously," I add. "Nicholas Zane, my new brother."

It feels weird to say that. I have Marly and Shane, but they aren't really my brother and sister and they don't live with us all the time. But the New Baby will live with us all the time. And he's actually related to me, really, like we have the same mother. I wonder if he'll look like me. I mean, I know I look like my Real Dad, and he's dead. And Nicholas won't look like my Real Dad. He might look like my New Dad, in which case he'll probably look like Marly. But if you think about it, he's like the link that joins me and Marly and Shane because he's half-related to both of us. Maybe he'll look like me with Marly's crazy red hair. Or maybe he'll look like Shane with my bad, stringy gross hair. Ugh. Poor baby.

We stop at 31 Flavours and I get my favourite, peanut-butter chocolate on a waffle cone. It is actually too cold to eat ice cream, and right away I get one of those ice cream headaches that you get from eating ice cream too fast or whatever. "Gah gah gah," I say to clear the pain out of my brain, and Marly copies me.

"Gah gah gah," she says, only she has a mouthful of strawberry ice cream that drips all over the seat of the car. I can see Jenny cringing, because she knows it's her job to clean it up, so I wipe it up for her. I mean, it's not fair that she has to do everything for us. Not really. Even though she did get to steal my bedroom.

When we get home, Jenny goes to put Shane to bed and Marly and I finish the *Welcome* sign. I add a picture of a sheep, just because. I don't know. It makes sense to me. After calling Grandma and the two of us talking forever, Jenny says it's too late to call my friends, so I tell her that I'm going to bed and instead I go into my room and start going through my dresser looking for things to pack for the weekend. Holy moly, I'm excited. It's dumb, but I am. I can't help it.

I should tell you that the last time we were at the cabin, it was snowing. Dad took us up there for my birthday in February and there was a crazy and scary blizzard. It was completely cool. What is up with the weather this year, anyway? I mean, the rain is just kersplashing down like crazy and it's making a patch of dampness on my bedroom floor. (I always have a window open or I feel like I can't breathe. I can't explain it, it's just the way I am.) Anyway, we had gone up there for a school project and we were going to look for gold that was buried there by this crazy old guy called Brother XII. Instead, we ended up breaking into someone's cabin and almost losing our boat and having to eat canned food like spaghetti and so on all mixed together. It was the best birthday ever. It doesn't sound fun, but it was. We even invented a club called the Gold Diggers Club. I wonder where my GDC sweatshirt is? I start going through drawers looking for it and when I find it, I put it on. The sleeves are totally too short, but it still looks okay.

Well, it looks dumb, to tell you the truth.

Why are my arms so long? I stare at myself in the mirror and then go cross-eyed to make my body go all distorted. I have the longest arms and legs in the world, like a daddy-long-legs. If I don't get to be an Olympic diver when I grow up, maybe I can work in the circus as Long-Arm-and-Leg-Girl. Just for fun, I do a handstand and accidentally kick over a bunch of books on the shelf. Normally, plenty of people (i.e. Mum and Dad) would come running when they heard such a ruckus, but they aren't here. It seems a bit weird to be alone in the house with just Jenny, to be frank. She's nice and everything, but she doesn't come running when there is a thud. I pick the books up and start flipping through them.

One of them is this really neat book on diving where they show you how many points each dive is worth and there are pictures of all the different steps of the dive. Diving is such a hard-to-explain thing because it happens so fast, it's not like you have time to go, "Okay, here is where I pull my knees in and here is where I twist around and point my toes." It's more like jump-up-bend-twist-squinch-pull-tuck-point-splash! all at once and almost without thinking about it. I mean, obviously you have to think about it or you would just belly-flop into the water. Come to think about it, I don't know how I do it without stopping in the middle and deciding what to do next. In a way, it reminds me of trying to learn French at school. It's impossible if you try to think in English and translate into French. You have to just skip the first step and think in French the first time. With diving, you just have to feel the dive and not think about it. In English or French. Well, I'm sure that doesn't make sense to you unless you're a diver, too.

I put the books away and start emptying out my drawers looking for summer stuff that fits me. I have lots of bathing suits that fit because of diving, natch. But all my shorts and stuff from last year are too small. For a second, I get kind of mad inside my head. Like normally my mum would have taken me shopping for summer clothes by now. I'm eleven-going-on-twelve, so I'm obviously growing and have to buy new clothes every season, and even Mum with her giant belly and constant sleeping has to have noticed that I'm suddenly a freakishly tall ape. I put on my favourite T-shirt from last summer and it's way too tight across the top and I start to cry for no real reason. I guess I just feel sad that I'm growing up and no one knows it. And also, what am I going to wear this weekend? The wind whips a big branch against the glass of my window and nearly scares me half to death. Maybe if it's windy, we won't be able to go. I kind of don't even want to go now that I realize I have nothing to wear. I know it sounds crazy but I have a feeling it's going to be super-hot this weekend, it being, of course, the First Weekend of Summer Holidays.

I ball up all the clothes that don't fit me and stuff them under the bed, which is no small feat because there is already a lot of crap under there. I have to use my feet to firmly push it all in and I hear a clattering when I do it, so there must have been some dishes underneath. Oops. Seriously, it's too scary for words under there. I hope I never have to clean it out.

I lie on my back on the floor for a few minutes, just thinking about everything and the whole world and the New Baby and Mum's stomach and math and going to the cabin and diving. I stretch myself out really long and point my toes. My favourite diver of all time, Laura Wilkinson, is like five foot six. I'm going to be six feet tall! I've never heard of any tall female divers. My life is ruined.

Okay, it's not ruined.

Well, it *is* ruined.

Or not.

I don't know. I start to bite my fingernails,

which I hardly ever do anymore, just because there isn't much else to do while lying on the floor. I bite too far down my pinky nail and it starts to bleed. Great, just great. I kind of think maybe I'll sleep on the floor tonight to make a point, but I'm not sure what the point is. I kind of realize that we didn't actually eat supper tonight. We — or at least, I — had pie and ice cream. I sit up and squinch in my belly. What if I get fat? Then I'll be both fat and tall. Then I totally won't be able to be a diver. Then what will I do? I'm too dumb to be a doctor.

I get up and sit at my desk and make a list of what I can be when I grow up if the Olympics thing doesn't work out for me. It looks like this:

What I Can Be When I Grow Up:
1.
2.
3.

Huh.

I guess maybe I shouldn't quit gymnastics — I need something to fall back on.

I crawl into bed in my clothes without brushing my teeth because I can't be bothered and no one told me to. It drives Mum crazy when I do that, when I say, "Well, no one told me to." She gets all exasperated and says, "No one should *have* to tell you!" I feel almost bad when I think of that, and think of getting up and brushing my teeth anyway, and to tell you the truth, they feel kind of gross from eating all that sugar, and drinking cola always makes me feel like I have little sweaters on my teeth, which is very unpleasant, as I'm sure you can imagine. But I don't do it. I'm being rebellious.

Then, just as I'm falling asleep, I have a great idea. I could join the circus! There is this really cool circus called Cirque du Soleil — which I happen to know means Circus of the Sun because they force-teach us French at school — which travels around. If you haven't seen it, you totally should. It's all flying through the air and gymnastics and stuff and there is one underwater show where my superior diving skills would come in really handy. I'm so excited by my idea that I can't sleep, so instead I go into Mum and Dad's room and take some of Mum's T-shirts to wear at the cabin. And shorts. She won't mind and it's not like she can fit into them anyway. It feels strange to be in their room when they aren't there. It sort of smells like them. Just because I can, I crawl into their bed and experiment with falling asleep, and it must totally work because next thing I know Jenny is waking me up and she's all freaked out because she couldn't find me in my own bed. It's morning! I had a really good sleep. It's weird how other people's beds are always more comfortable than your own.

"Don't worry," I tell her. "I just wanted to sleep in here. Mum said I could." Which is a lie but it makes Jenny feel better, and so that makes it sort of okay, even though it probably isn't okay according to God or whatever you believe in.

"Lying is never okay!" Dad always says. But I think he's wrong. I think if you tell someone something that cheers them up, it's okay.

"I've got your breakfast on the table, and you have to hurry or you'll be late!" Jenny says. And my heart starts to beat faster in a *pitter-pat* of excitement because it's the First Day of the Last Week of School, it's Countdown to Summer, and the New Baby, that little sheep NZ, is coming home with my mum today, and, oh, lots of reasons that I don't even have time to tell you about right now because the sun is beaming into the room like crazy and it looks like it's going to be a perfect, hot summer day.

I push Treasure off me — he somehow fell asleep all nestled up in my elbow — and I try to rub his hair off the bed. He meows like he's mad, but I know he isn't because as soon as I'm out of bed, he starts slinking around my legs like he always does. I nearly trip over him and break my leg as I hurry back to my room to get ready.

I guess that storm cleared the whole sky off and it even smells like summer, with the grassy smells and the hot pavement smells and everything. And for the first time in a while, I feel crazy happy. I even hug Mealy Marly on my way out the door, that's how happy I am. And trust me, that never happens. Well, almost never.

chapter 3

As soon as I get to the schoolyard, Felicia and Montana come running over to me. Felicia is wearing new shoes, which are *really* cute. I wish I could wear cute shoes, but I can't. I'm too tall for "cute." It makes me mad, to be honest.

"I like your shoes!" I tell her.

"What?" she says. "Oh, my shoes." She wiggles her foot. "Okay, but never mind! Tell us about the baby! Is it a boy or a girl?"

"It's a boy!" I say. "It's a boy!" I don't know why I say it twice. Then I say it again. "It's a boy!" I'm like a stuck CD.

"A boy!" squeals Montana. "I'm so excited for you!"

"Me, too!" I say, even though I don't know if I am. I mean, I am, but I'm not. It's hard to explain. It's like people want me to be more excited than I am so I can't really tell how excited I am because I'm pretending to be as excited as I'm supposed to be.

"Does he cry all the time?" says Felicia.

"No!" I say. "Yes!"

"What?" she says.

"I don't know," I say. "They don't get out of the hospital until this afternoon. But I'm pretty sure he will! Cry all the time, I mean." I giggle.

They just kind of look at me, like they need more information or like I'm talking like someone who is nutso. So I try to get myself together and say, in a normal voice, "He's cute. He has black hair and blue eyes. And he's super small. Smaller than I would have thought." I hold up my hands.

"Tiny!" says Montana. Then she says, "I can't wait to meet him!"

"I know!" says Felicia. "Me, too!"

"Well," I say, "you can meet him soon. But he doesn't do much. I mean, he's a baby."

"I loooove babies," says Montana. Her eyes are shining. Is she tearing up? I swear I don't understand her sometimes. She's very emotional. On the other hand, maybe she's normal and *I'm* not. Is there something wrong with me? I mean, I think babies are great but I don't *love* them. They just are what they are.

"Totally," I agree, just for the sake of agreeing. And then the bell goes, which saves me from saying very much else.

It's very hard to concentrate in class on what Mrs. Witless is saying when the sun is filling up the whole room. You can even smell it a little bit, like all the dust in the air is hotter than usual. It seems as if it would taste like summer even. It also seems wrong that we are here at all.

I'd forgotten, what with all the excitement, but we're going to the museum this afternoon, so we won't be here long enough for anything she's saying to make any difference. Why is she trying to *teach* us things? She must be crazy.

Instead of paying attention, I use my favourite gel pens to draw a map for Felicia and Montana to try to make them guess what I'm inviting them for this weekend. I fold the note up really small and ping it at Montana's head, but she totally doesn't feel it and it falls on the floor. I don't want Tim the Nose Blower or anyone else to pick it up, so I have to throw a pen in the same direction so I have a reason to be getting it myself. Naturally, I get caught.

"Carly!" yells Mrs. Witless, like her hair is on fire. "What are you doing?"

"I dropped my pen?" I say.

"You dropped your pen in front of you by three metres?" she says. She sighs like her head is about to explode and massages her temples. She's very overly dramatic. "Honestly, Carly. Go to the office."

I stick out my tongue, which is quite probably a huge mistake. She makes a grimacing look at me.

Sometimes I forget that Mrs. Witless is a real person. I wonder what Mr. Witless is like. I wonder what their house looks like. She probably has a lot of cats, and not in a good way. The only way to have a cat is to have one of them, like Treasure, and not fourteen. Fourteen is crazy.

"Carly!" she says.

"What?" I say.

"Get going," she says. Her face is quite red. I can hear Montana giggle.

"Sorr-y," I say. "I mean, I am sorry."

"Carly," she sighs.

"My mum had a baby yesterday," I say, by way of explanation.

"Fine," she says. "Is it a boy or a girl?"

"It's a boy," I say.

"That's nice!" she says, suddenly beaming at me. Why do babies make people so happy? I make like I'm going to sit down again and she yells, "But that doesn't mean you don't have to go to the office, Carly!"

Huh.

I pick up my pencil case for no real reason, and carry it with me to the principal's office. I don't know why I'm bringing it. It's not like I'll be expected to write anything down while getting in trouble. Lately I feel like I'm always getting in trouble. It's very hard to be eleven sometimes. You have no idea. Unless you yourself are also eleven, in which case, you know. Obviously. I'm looking forward a great deal to being twelve, as I'm sure you are too, if you're eleven. You know what I mean.

I get to the principal's office and his door is closed so I sit down and make small talk with the secretary, who is named Daisy or Rose or Tulip or some other kind of flower that I can't remember.

"Lovely day," I say.

"Hmmph," she says. She looks at me over her half-moon glasses. Outside of schools and old people's homes, you never see those glasses anywhere. I wonder if you have to get them from a special mail-order catalogue.

"Can I try on your glasses?" I ask politely.

"Absolutely not," she says. She has something black on her tooth. I'm about to tell her this when I realize that she doesn't actually have something black *on* her tooth, she just has a black tooth. A black tooth! I'm sure she didn't have a black tooth last time I was here. Do teeth just suddenly turn black? Has she noticed?

It's horrifying.

When you hold it up against the horror of having a black tooth, I realize that my life is not so difficult. Just because I have no bedroom and am freakishly tall and have to take Math for Stunted Brains, I'm officially not the unluckiest person alive. It's possible that Rose or Daisy or Lily or

Petunia is the unluckiest person alive. I smile at her to be nice and open my pencil case to offer her a piece of gum, which backfires horribly because all my pencils and felt pens and glitter pens and gel pens fall out and roll all over the floor.

"Please sit down," she says, in a voice that says, "Sit down right now or there'll be heck to pay."

"I have to pick up my pens," I say. I feel a bit embarrassed. I just wanted to give her gum! Pens are everywhere! It's like my pencil case exploded.

"Fine," she says and glares at me. Really, I was just being nice. It was an accident! I don't understand the hostility of the adults in this school. Honestly.

I start crawling around on the floor — which, by the way, is not very clean — and picking up pens and stuffing them back in my case. There are dust bunnies down here the size of small bears. I'm not kidding — these are dust *dinosaurs*. They practically dwarf me. I'm a bit afraid they are going to start rumbling around like tumbleweeds in Western movies. Just when I think I'm almost finished, I see my favourite purple gel pen over in the far corner behind a cobweb. I'm just trying to get the pen without touching the cobweb when an alarmingly mobile dust dinosaur comes rocketing towards my nose. Naturally, this makes me sneeze, and as I go to sit up, I bang my forehead on the sticky-out metal thing on the bottom of the chair I was crawling under. Really hard. So hard that I feel like my eyes are blurring up. I kind of fall back on the floor and I can feel blood — blood! — trickling from my face.

"Aaah!" I yell.

"What?" someone says, peering down at me. "What happened to you?"

"I've hit my head," I say. I squint at the person, who is clearly not the principal or the secretary. My hand is clamped firmly over what must be an appallingly bad injury. The person talking seems to be some sort of boy but he's wearing a tie. What kind of a boy wears a tie? "Who are you?" I say.

"That's not very polite," he says, "when I was just going to help you up."

"What's not polite?" I say. "I was just asking who you are."

"It's not what you say," he says, crouching down enough that I can see that he's just a regular eleven-year-old boy (or looks like one). "It's how you say it." He has an unusual accent.

"Are you from Australia?" I ask, holding my hand tightly over the blood because it's a bit embarrassing to be lying there bleeding in front of an Australian boy. I'm very interested in Australia because we almost moved there and then didn't.

"Don't be daft," he says. "I'm English."

"Well, we're all *English*," I say. "If we weren't, we'd be speaking another language."

He makes a snorting sound that might be laughter. "I'm *from* England," he says.

"Oh," I say. "Nice." I'm still lying on the floor. My hand feels sticky. Probably there is a river of blood pouring into my hair.

"Er . . . " he says, "cheers." And he walks away.

Well, if he isn't the rudest boy I've ever seen in all my life. I struggle into a sitting position to flag down the secretary's attention. *Cheers!* I don't even have a drink in my hand, and if I did, I'm sure I wouldn't "cheers" him. Hmmmph. But the secretary's gone. Where did she go? I rub my eye and realize my hand (and now my eye) has blood on (in) it. Gross.

"Argh!" I scream, loud enough for, well, pretty much anyone to hear. The principal sticks his head out the door.

"Oh my goodness," he says. "You're bleeding!"

"Yes, I am," I say. I'm still holding onto my purple gel pen, which I put carefully into the pencil case.

"Get up!" he says, "Go to the nurse."

"Huh," I say. I try to get up, but my legs have gone all rubber-bandy. "I need some help," I say.

He reaches over to help me like I'm a particularly rotten piece of fruit that he doesn't want to touch. Figures. I mean, you can't really count on the milk of human kindness, can you? My grandma always says that, and she's right. Revelry *is* dead! Or whatever.

He kind of half drags me down the hall. I'm very satisfied to see little plops of blood falling on the linoleum. Now they'll have to clean the floor, I think. I don't know why I care about this, but I do. I mean, I know I'm a bit of a slob sometimes, but cleanliness is very important to me. I'm a bit disappointed that he didn't call an ambulance and have me rushed to the hospital. Not that I like hospitals, but it might have been an adventure.

"Hi, Carly," the nurse says, seeing me. She knows me from last winter when I jammed the pointy part of that geometry thing into my hand and fainted. What a piece of work she must think I am.

"Hi," I say. "How's your boyfriend?"

She looks at me funny. "He's fine." She doesn't have an accent, even though she once told me that she's French Canadian. Try as I might, I can't remember her name. I'm terrible with names. Awful. Which is weird because I'm always thinking about names, as in what names are good and what ones are bad. When you think about my friends, they all pretty much have good names. Montana is a great name. Her parents chose the name by throwing a dart at the map. They were going to move to Montana but they liked it here better, so they used the name instead. Felicia is also a great name. It's so pretty. And Sam's name is good because it suits her.

"Carly?" the nurse says. "What's up?"

I decide that I think her name is Stephanie. It sort of feels right.

"Stephanie," I say, "can you patch up my head?"

"Hmm," she says.

The principal kind of stomps away like he's annoyed that I've taken up so much of his time. On the plus side, he didn't have a chance to get mad at me about the note or the tongue-sticking-out incident, which cheers me up immeasurably. Also, I enjoy getting medical attention. It makes me feel hugged.

Stephanie, or whatever her name is (she didn't correct me, so I must be right) pats my head with a wet cloth to get the blood off.

"It's not much of a cut," she says. "You don't need stitches or anything. Heads just bleed a lot."

"Oh," I say. I'm the tiniest bit disappointed because stitches are cool.

"I'll put a Band-Aid on it," she says. "Do you want to choose?" She holds out a selection of Band-Aids with Disney characters on them. Clearly she has mistaken me for someone who is six years old.

"I don't care," I say, trying to imply that I'm too old to care and that I require only a sophisticated, non-patterned Band-Aid. Apparently she inter-prets this to mean that I want to have a giant Little Mermaid perched on my forehead. Huh. I remember her as being much more cool than that.

"Thanks," I say sarcastically.

"No problem," she says. "Now get back to class."

Well! What a letdown. Not that I wanted to get in trouble *or* get stitches, but I wander back to the classroom feeling like something was supposed to happen that didn't. Only the thing is that when I get to the classroom, the English Boy, who may or may not be cute, is sitting in my seat.

"Get out of my seat," I say loudly, and then I blush. I can't explain the blushing, so don't ask.

"CARLY," says Mrs. Witless. "You can't just interrupt the entire class."

"Mrs. Whitfield," I say. "Please. I'm sorry. I've just had a terrible head injury and now there is a boy in my seat."

"That boy is named Nigel," she says. "And he's new to our school, so please try to be nice to him. You can sit at the table at the back."

"What?" I say. "I'm being bumped from my own desk?" I feel like crying. My Little Mermaid Band-Aid throbs. I've been ousted from my own seat in the classroom. After being bumped from my new bedroom, this is really like the final insult.

"Yes," she says. "And if you interrupt the class one more time, you're getting detention." Felicia shoots me a sympathetic look. I stomp to the back of the classroom just so everyone knows how miserable I am. I'm still holding onto my pencil case. Why? I don't even know. I just am. The New Boy laughs just loud enough that I can hear it. Well. I used to think that Tim the Nose Blower was about the worst person in the world, but now I know I'm wrong. Nigel the New Boy is by far the worst. I glower at him as if to say, "A curse on you and your family!" But it probably doesn't work as well as I hoped, what with the giant sparkling bandage above my right eye.

By the time afternoon finally rolls around and we drag ourselves out to the bus to go to the museum, I'm in such a sour mood that I almost forget to tell Montana and Felicia about going to the cabin. Luckily, we all get to sit together at the back of the bus, so all is not lost. And it's so super-sunny outside that I really need sunglasses, which of course I forgot to bring. I want to tell them about the obnoxious New Boy and the experience I had in the principal's office, which I've already told them once at lunch, but they don't want to hear it again. In fact, all they seem to want to know about is the New *Baby*.

Frankly, I think the New *Boy* is almost more interesting. I mean, nothing has happened with the New Baby yet. It's not like there has been an incident. Secretly, I'm kind of mad, but I try to be nice and play along.

"Tell us more about what he looks like!" says Felicia. "What kind of nose does he have? What are his eyes like?"

"All babies have blue eyes," I tell her, like she should know — which is a bit mean, really, since I didn't know myself until that baby class I was forced to take. It's probably like my duty and responsibility to teach everyone else these important things instead of being snappish. I try harder. "And his hair is black but it's just the hair that he's born with. It will probably fall out and then some other colour hair will come in. I don't know about his nose. What kinds of noses are there?"

"I don't know," she says, giggling. "I guess just big and little."

"Hmm," I say. I can't exactly picture his nose, to be honest. "It's little. Everything about him is little."

"Oh!" Montana says, leaning forward in the seat. "I'm so jealous that you have a baby to play with."

"It's not all fun and games," I say sagely. Of course, the baby isn't home from the hospital yet so I don't actually know. Maybe it will be fun and games! Maybe I'm misjudging the whole situation! But I doubt it. "Babies are SO much work."

"How do you know?" asks Montana. "I thought you said he wasn't home yet."

"Oh," I say. "Well, um, no, he's not home yet. But I took a class."

"Oh," she says. "I'm sorry about your head — that must hurt."

"It does hurt," I say. "It *kills.*" Which is not untrue. It does sort of throb.

"Yuck," says Felicia. "Poor you. And the New Boy was so mean to you, too."

"Yes," I agree. "Can you believe he didn't even help me up? Huh."

But no one's listening anymore because we've pulled up to the museum. Everyone piles out of the bus and through the big wooden doors. Right away we all split up, even though we aren't supposed to get separated. We hide in this big Native Canadian Longhouse on the second floor as soon as we can find it, which is harder than you think. The museum is very big.

The longhouse is neat and it echoes. I like to chant in there and pretend that we're living out in the woods and eating animals that we skinned ourselves. I get so excited about the museum (I know it's lame and I've been there a million times, but I still like it) that I forget *again* to tell them about the cabin. It's only as I'm walking home from school that I remember.

D'oh! I'm so forgetful sometimes. Maybe there's something wrong with my brain. That would explain a lot of things. I hope I don't have a tumour or worse.

I call everyone right away when I get home. Like

I just run in the door and call them and I talk on the phone about what we're going to do and then I call Sam because she goes to a different school and invite her and I realize I've been home for an hour or maybe more and no one has even said hi to me. In fact, there is no one home.

Where is everyone?

I look around in all the rooms and it's all empty, which is creepy because the front door was unlocked. Maybe something happened? Right away I start getting scared and running around the house like crazy, which makes the dogs bark but does not make the following people appear:

1. Mum
2. Dad
3. Jenny
4. Marly
5. Shane
6. The New Baby a.k.a. NZ

It reminds me of one of those movies where maybe the whole family goes away and the kid is left alone and then burglars break in and he accidentally nearly tortures them to death. It was supposed to be funny, but I found it a little unsettling. Frankly, I don't relish the idea of being home alone with burglars. I'm just about to freak out completely when I see a big note on the table that says that Dad is bringing Mum home and everyone else is at the park.

Everyone!

I guess I'm not part of "everyone." Huh. I'm like the person who is not Everyone but Someone Else. That's just great. That's a fine bucket of fish. I feel this peculiar floaty feeling in my head, as though I can feel that I'm turning invisible. Like in a comic book. I don't exist! This makes me feel almost like crying but I don't. Instead, I get a good bit mad. I stomp my way down to the park with Blue and Roo in tow. You'd think if *everyone* was going for a walk, they'd take the dogs with them. I'm just about there when I see them coming towards me. Jenny kind of runs at me and grabs me and says, "Carly, what happened to your head? You poor thing, we were worried when you didn't come for our picnic so we packed it up and we were coming home to find you."

"Hmmph," I say. To tell you the truth, I still feel a bit choked up and my head hurts and the sun is squimping off my eyes and hurting them, so I blink really hard and say, "Thanks."

When we get home, Dad is helping Mum out of the car and the New Baby — who I'm going to try to think of as Nicholas Zane, but it's hard — is nowhere to be seen.

"Where's the baby?" I yell, suddenly worried that my lacklustre interest in him has somehow made him vanish. I know it doesn't make sense, but it's the first thing I thought of.

"Shhh," Mum says, and points. The New Baby, I mean Nicholas Zane, I mean NZ, is sleeping in the car seat. He's just so small, it's like he's hardly even there. He's all slumped over in a way that looks, frankly, very painful. I'm sure that can't be good for the little guy. Dad hoists out his whole seat and plops it down on the lawn. The baby's eyes are tightly shut.

I plop down next to him and stare. "Hey," I say. "I'm your big sister, Carly." His eyes flip open but he doesn't look like he's looking at me. He looks like he's sleeping with his eyes open. "I'm your sister," I say again, and I think I see him wink at me. I mean, I know that babies can't wink, but I swear it looked like he did.

Huh. Maybe he's not so dull after all.

"What did you do at school today?" Mum says when we finally get her and her bags and the other kids and the baby and everyone inside. She's lying down on the couch, like walking in from the car has made her sleepy. I try not to stare at her stomach. Really, it's quite interesting. The baby was in there! Now it isn't!

"Well?" she says.

So I tell her about Nigel the New Boy and the Terrible Head Injury and while I'm telling her, I realize that I just don't feel so mad anymore. It wasn't the best day in the world, but hey, it wasn't the worst either, was it? At least I don't have black teeth. That would be horrible. Why would that happen anyway? I'm going to start flossing every day.

I swear it.

Then the baby starts making this mewing sound and Mum starts to open her shirt so I go running up to my (the New Baby's) room to do something that doesn't involve watching the baby eat. I mean, really, some things are just too much.

chapter 4

The funny thing is that the week — the last, end-less week — of school goes by very fast. I think maybe it's because I'm so tired from all that is going on at home, it takes on a bit of a dreamlike feeling, except not a dream, more like a nightmare featuring Nigel the New Boy.

He is my new nemesis. That's what Mum said when I tried to explain to her how awful he was and how insane it was that he joined school in the last week in the first place and how he tortured me by laughing and making snarky British-sounding remarks about the goose egg on my head. In case you are wondering, my terrible head wound got strangely swollen during the night after it happened and resulted in my forehead looking large-ish and crooked. Not pretty. Not that I care about being pretty in front of Nigel anyway. Give me a break. He's so weird and his clothes are all a little bit strange. I'm sure they are very nice clothes when you are in Europe but when you are in Canada, they just seem unusual and, well, I have to say it: dorky.

A nemesis, Mum says, is like a mortal enemy. Like The Joker is to Batman or Superman or whichever movie that guy was in with the big stretchy head. She also suggested that maybe I had a *crush* on Nigel and that he wasn't actually my enemy, but that for some insanc reason, I liked him, which is so ridiculous I won't even think about it for one more second.

Hmmph. Honestly, I forgive her for being so blind to the truth — that I hate Nigel quite a lot — because she is very tired from all the crying and eating that NZ is doing all the time.

Anyway, somehow — and I don't know how, so don't ask — I make it through the very last week of school and the first week of NZ (who is sleeping in my mum and dad's room, so hasn't actually booted me out to the garage yet, which is one good thing). It wasn't the worst week of my life but *plenty* went wrong. For example, when we went to the beach for Beach Day, I got stung by a bee on my rear end. I'd tell you how it happened but I'm too embarrassed.

Okay, I'll tell you, but don't laugh.

I sat on the bee.

Are you happy? I *sat* on a *bee.* And naturally, it got mad and it stung me and my bum got all swollen up until it was the size of a pumpkin. I'm not exaggerating. It was about a thousand times bigger than the goose egg on my forehead, though, which is good in a way. It balanced it out.

Also, my nose got sunburned. I was wearing sunscreen! I was! Why does the nose burn more easily than the rest of the body? If you ask me, it's a very poor design. You'd think that when human beings were being created the first time around, God (or whoever) would have said, "Well, let's make all the sticky-outy bits burn-proof." But no. So to summarize, I have a lump on my forehead, a swollen buttock (is buttock the singular of buttocks?) and a red, peeling nose.

Also (and I wasn't going to mention this, but I sort of feel like it now that I'm listing bad things), I had a really, really terrible diving practice on Wednesday. I guess there is a small possibility that I am over-thinking the whole thing. You know, thinking too much about how all of a sudden I'm so tall and how gymnastics is suddenly all wonky. For example, I was on the 5-metre spring-board, which is my favourite of all favourites and usually one that I have no trouble with, doing a dive I've done a kajillion billion times, and think-ing, Hey, if I'm much taller suddenly than I used to be, I bet I could accidentally kick the diving board on my way by after the big jump up, and then the rest of my dive would probably be wrecked! So that's what happened. Like ten times in a row. I may have been so frustrated that I cried. And Jon, my coach, was getting pretty antsy with me and asking me what was wrong and to pull it together and I just got more and more upset and now I'm pretty sure that I've wrecked everything as far as diving is concerned. Jon thinks I'm an idiot, which is nothing new because earlier this year I suddenly and randomly got scared of the platform. Obviously there is something very wrong with me and he can see that. Oh, boy. I'm sure he's thinking, There's no way Carly is going to the Olympics! She can't even do a forward one and a half off the 5-metre. What a dud!

So I suppose there is an outside chance that I'll never dive again. Maybe I'll quit diving, as well as gymnastics. Not that anyone has paid any notice to the fact that I've quit gymnastics. This is because of the following:

1. The New Baby
2. The New Baby
3. The New Baby

Basically, the New Baby, or BaaBaa, as I've decided to call him (Nicholas Zane . . . NZ . . . New Zealand . . . sheep . . . Get it?), cries all the time. (When he cries it sounds a bit like *Baaaa Baaaa* too.) *All* the time. I think he does it in his sleep. The end result of this is that everyone is so tired that no one cares about anyone else, anything else, or even themselves. Everyone is staggering around in a daze. You should see my mum. I swear, she hasn't even bothered to shower since she got home from the hospital. She's beginning to look an awful lot like a witch. And she smells! Just a bit, but you don't want to get too close. Also, she is spending an amount of time crying. Between her crying and BaaBaa baahing, well, it's enough to make me cry, to tell you the honest to Pete truth. Shane and Marly have gone to stay with their mum temporarily, and/or until we can get the house completely soundproofed. It was my understanding when I took the course that babies slept eighteen hours a day. Oooh, boy, that's funny.

Ha dee ha ha.

I'm pretty much going to write an email to the people who run that course to say, "What are you thinking? You can't lie to people! Babies never sleep! They cry all the time! And they aren't that cute, really, are they? They stink! And poo! And barf!" I'm fairly confident that they could completely get rid of the whole "teen pregnancy problem" they are always rattling on about in health class by just showing people what babies are really like.

I'm serious.

Anyway, I made it through the week alive. I guess that's something.

And now it's Friday. Friday! The Last Day of the Last Week of School! Just as I'm walking towards the car outside the schoolyard, Nigel comes running up to me and says, "Jolly good meeting you!" which I'm sure is Nigel-speak for something very rude. Probably he was being sarcastic. Among other things he said this week, while laughing, was, "How's the weather up there, Stretch?" and "I'll bet you're good at basketball!" Ha. Ha. So funny I forgot to laugh.

So I say, "I'm sure," and step around him. Luckily, Dad is there honking his horn like mad. Can he not see me? I mean, seriously. *I'm right here.*

"Dad," I say as I get in the car, "that's jolly loud." The car is fully loaded with all the cabin stuff because we're leaving super early tomorrow and Dad wanted to get ready "early." A sleeping bag slips down from the pile of junk in the back and nearly suffocates me. I wrestle it off. I love sleeping bags. I know it's weird, but they are just so great and rustly and cabin-y.

"Good day?" he says half-heartedly. He has bags under his eyes that are so big they look like plums.

"No," I say pointedly. "Jolly bad."

"Good," he says, which tells me that he's not listening. It actually wasn't a bad day anyway so I'm sort of glad I don't have to explain. At least today I didn't get stung by a bee or stabbed in the eye with a javelin (not that this has happened to me, but I've heard that it happened to someone at this school once a long time ago). *And* I don't have to see Nigel again until September. And I collected a million autographs in my yearbook and managed to scribble out my picture in almost everyone's book with a black marker because it's the worst picture you've ever seen in your life. Really. I look like a buck-toothed, pre-pimple-faced, bad-haired freak. I'm sure it was bad lighting. Probably the photographer didn't like me.

Anyway. I stuff my yearbook under the seat. Mum says I'll like having a yearbook to look back on when I'm old. Which is all very well, except that there are no grossly awful pictures of her in *her* old yearbooks. I should add also that Nigel wrote something very strange in my book. He wrote, *I'm sure I'll see a lot of you around.* What does that mean?

Weirdo.

When we get home, Mum is asleep and so is the baby. Jenny is making us an early dinner of tofu scramble and veggies, which she pours all this sauce on to make it taste good. We're just about done eating when Mum wakes up and sleepily wanders into the room. She's had a shower, which is a good sign. She seems really happy that we're going to the cabin because she keeps saying, "I'm so glad you're going to get the mooring done!"

Dad keeps saying, "Are you sure?" which is getting pretty repetitive, for Pete's sake. She's sure! She's sure!

For once BaaBaa isn't sobbing, so I get to hold him a bit before bed. I haven't really held him that much. It seems like he's always on Mum for one reason or another and I don't like to change him. It makes me nervous. So she pretty much does everything. And Jenny, of course. And Grandma is coming tomorrow after we leave, so that's good. She'll help, too. They can all change diapers. Just when I'm thinking how good he smells and I'm sniffing his head a bit, he lets out the most enormous fart you've ever heard and practically explodes out of his diapers. I hand him back pretty quickly, I can tell you that.

I lie awake for most of the night because I'm so seriously excited I can't settle my own head down long enough to catch onto a dream. When I do sleep, I half-dream about babies crying. Probably this is because the baby was crying. When I wake up in the morning, I'm a darn bit more tired than I'd like to be but I don't complain. Mum is all teary and Dad is in complete guilt overdrive.

"Go! Go!" she says.

And we do.

Without saying much, Dad and I drive towards the marina where he keeps the boat. Felicia's parents are going to drop off the other girls, which is good because there certainly isn't any room in here with us, the stuff and the dog. Blue keeps slathering in my ear. We aren't bringing Roo because of her hip and because Mum said that she needed Roo for protection and company. Poor Roo — no sleep for her this weekend. Roo seems very confused about the baby. She keeps sniffing him like she can't decide whether to eat him or play with him or run away. Which is a darn sight better than Treasure, who is *sure* he wants to eat him. He has to be kept out. He's acting very very strangely. Mum says he's jealous.

"Well," says Dad, breaking the silence, "at least we'll get some sleep this weekend!" And he laughs like it's the funniest thing in the world. It's possible that he's hysterical from lack of sleep himself. I have no idea. I have no experience with this sort of thing. He sort of makes a hiccupping snorting sound, like he's trying to stop.

"Right," I say. I just hope he doesn't start crying. Frankly, I can't much handle any more crying at this point. In the back of my mind, I'm calculating how many trips up the hill it will take to get all the stuff that's crammed in our car up to the cabin. The cabin is at the top of a giant, steep slope and because there are no cars and no driveways, you pretty much have to carry everything up on your back. It dawns on me that this is the reason why Dad invited four eleven-year-old girls.

We may not be much good at scuba diving with concrete mooring blocks and chains and all that stuff that he has to do, but we can *carry* things. We're like donkeys in the Grand Canyon that we saw in a film in Grade Four.

"Huh," I say.

"What is it?" he says.

"Nothing," I say. I mean, I don't want to complain about having the chance to go to the cabin on the first weekend of summer holidays. "I was thinking about math."

"I used to *love* math when I was a kid," he says.

Now why do adults always say things like this to kids? Obviously, I *hate* math and I'm *horrible* at it. How am I supposed to react to this revelation? I'm very happy that he *loved* math, in that I don't care. "Wow," I say, because it's all that I can think of. "Neat."

"What I mean is that I can probably help you with it," he says.

"Great," I say. Meaning "what*ever.*" I roll my eyes and glower out the window. There are fourteen (I counted them) men on bicycles racing down the shoulder of the highway. They're wearing yellow jerseys and look like demented insects with their helmets on and their funny hunched-over backs. I stick out my tongue at them.

I just don't want to think about math this weekend. Why did I bring up a conversation about math? Sometimes I have no idea why my brain does what it does. It makes no sense to me. I was just sitting here thinking about the cabin and all of a sudden, POW!, math jumps in and wrecks my mood.

I slump down in the seat and begin tying my shoelaces in elaborate knots like they use in sailing. My Real Dad taught me to tie fancy knots when I was very little, like five years old. Whenever I'm feeling a bit blue, I tie things in knots. (Well, sometimes I do. Other times I just go ahead and feel blue.) Honestly, I have no idea why *math* is considered by the school to be more important than knot tying. Why isn't there a knot class? Knot tying is much more useful (obviously) and I'm *good* at it. If the school offered knot tying as a class, I'd get an *A*, and usually the only thing I get an *A* in is PE (and blood type). Or lately, anyway. I think I was smarter when I was younger, like last year.

Dad looks over at me. "We're going to have a good weekend," he says.

"Okay," I say.

We pull into the parking lot of the marina. From the car, I can already see the other girls waiting at the top of the ramp in their matching GDC sweatshirts. For a second, I feel a plip-plop of jealousy because I couldn't get mine to fit, but I just pull my perfectly good Dolphin Diving Club sweatshirt around me and get out of the car to say hi. Every-one seems really excited and they're all talking at once and they have a bunch of stuff. What's real-ly great is that Felicia's mum has a cake pan in her hand, which means she's giving us one of her famous carrot cakes with cream-cheese icing. My favourite! Yum.

"Have fun, girls," she says, getting into her car. "Be careful!"

Felicia kind of rolls her eyes, which is funny if you know her because Felicia is totally not an eye roller. She's more of a smile-and-nodder, if you know what I mean. She is the most polite person of all time. She always says please and thank you about ten times, even for stupid stuff that doesn't warrant manners, like if someone was stepping on her toe, she'd probably say, "Could you please get off my toe? Thank you." She's never rude. I've never seen her stick out her tongue at Mrs. Wit-less, for example.

"I'm *so* excited," she says. "I wish we could get there right away."

"Me, too," I say.

"Where's your Club shirt?" says Sam.

"Oh," I say. Suddenly I don't want to say that it's too small. "Um, I couldn't find it."

"Too bad!" she says.

"Yeah," I say, trying to change the subject. "Let's get this stuff to the boat!"

Dad starts emptying out the car and Blue starts barking. He barks when he's excited. Also when he's nervous, hungry, has to pee or is mad. In summary, Blue barks constantly.

Finally, after forever, we get all the stuff to the boat and set off for the cabin.

Seriously, getting ready to go to the cabin takes a *million* hours. There has to be a better way. Some of the people at the cabin take a plane to get there, a sea plane, and they land in the bay where we like to dive off the rocks. If I were that rich, I'd totally take a plane. In fact, maybe when I grow up, I'll get my pilot's license and fly myself to the cabin and surprise people by visiting! Such as Mum and Dad, and of course Nicholas Zane, who will still be a kid when I'm an adult.

I'm thinking about this as we plow through the waves. It's really hard to talk on the boat because the engine is so noisy, but I can see Sam whispering something to Montana. What are they whispering about? Right away, I get worried that they are whispering about me, so I look out to sea and pretend not to care. I think that if something bothers you, you should just pretend it doesn't and if you pretend long enough then it becomes true. You should try this. I put a smile on my face because it also works if you are pretending to be happy.

I love being on the boat with the wind whipping

through our hair and stuff, and I hope I remembered to put sunscreen on because the thing with boats is that you don't feel how hot the sun is, even though it's only June, and next thing you know you are burned to a crisp, like a piece of bacon, and then what? And it's not like I'm not already burned. I fish around in my backpack and find some zinc and put it on my nose in a stripe. Felicia giggles. "You look like someone from a tribe!" she yells over the sound of the motor.

I give her some and she does some lines on her face. It looks totally funny. Then the other girls do, too. After that, we kind of settle back to just stare at the water because, for real, it's too hard to hear anything. I spend some time thinking about my mum and BaaBaa Nicholas Zane. I wonder what they're doing? I wonder if he went right back to sleep when we left? I hope so. She needs some sleep. Then I stop thinking about mum and start thinking about the last week of school and about how Nigel kept saying mean — or just weird — things to me. If I were into that sort of thing, I might think he was cute, but I'm not and he isn't. Take note of that! I do *not* think he is cute. Really.

Think about it: when I sat on the bee, he laughed to beat the band. I thought he was going to fall over, he laughed so hard. Who laughs at other people's hardships? I'll tell you who! Mean

People, that's who. And he's a Mean One all right. I just hope he isn't in my class next year. What are the odds?

The odds are actually one in two because there are only two Grade Six classes. Well. I wish he would stop popping into my head, for Pete's sake. It's driving me crazy. "Go *away*, Nigel," I say out loud. Then I'm embarrassed. What if someone heard me? Why am I talking out loud to Nigel when he isn't here?

I make no eye contact with the girls, just in case, and I push my sunglasses up my nose and watch the islands going by. There are rich people's houses all along the shores of most of them. I always like to imagine what I would do if the boat were to sink, where I would swim to. I would probably hope to choose a place with a hot tub to warm up in after I got to shore because the water is very very cold here. I mean, obviously, I'd always pick a close one and just hope for the best. It's hard to swim in a life jacket though, I've tried. So I guess what would really happen is that I'd bob around in the water for rescue. No hot tub, probably. I'm thinking about that and looking at the water when I see something really startling.

"Shark!" I scream. Because just off our port side (that's the left side of the boat, in case you don't know; "starboard" is right, which sounds much better than "right," if you want my opinion) there is a huge triangular dorsal fin! It's not like it could be a porpoise. It's enormous!

"What?" says Dad.

"Shark!" I scream again, but it's gone. I swear I saw it. The other girls are all excited.

"Was it really a shark?" Montana yells.

"Yes!" I say, looking frantically around in the water. I'm both scared and not scared of sharks. If by that, I mean terrified. I should tell you that I saw the rerun of an old movie very recently, called *Jaws*, which may have ruined my life. It was *extremely* terrifying. There was a time when I would have seen a fin and thought, "Whale!" or "Dolphin!" or "Porpoise!" But now I just assume it's a shark that wants to bite off my leg.

I didn't mean to watch that dumb movie anyway. Really, it's Nicholas Zane's fault because he was distracting Mum from stopping me from watching "inappropriate shows" on TV. I had my eyes shut through most of the movie, but I looked up at just the wrong time and saw a giant shark eating a person. It was the grossest thing ever. I wish now that I'd changed the channel. How hard would that have been? Huh. Stupid.

"There are no sharks around here," Dad says.

Well, now, I happen to know that that isn't true. Of *course* there are sharks. The sharks swim around the whole ocean. It's not like they get to the border between Canada and the rest of the world and swim away, saying, "Oh, that's Canada! We *never* go there!" Right.

"I wish I'd seen that fin," says Sam. "It would have made a good picture." She sounds like she really does.

Sam, as I've mentioned before, is very tough and adventurous. She has her camera in her lap and she holds it up and looks through it at the sea. She is very into picture taking all of a sudden. It's her new "thing." They have a photography club at her school and she's like the head person of the club. I can't understand it. It was so sudden! One day she was just regular Sam and now she's Sam-with-a-camera all the time. I think she even likes picture taking better than diving. Last time we dove together, she took a picture of me in the worst dive I've ever done. I was kind of mad, to tell you the honest to goodness truth.

Then I was talking to her on the phone last week and she took a picture of herself talking on the phone and emailed it to me with the heading, *This is me, talking to you on the phone.* I think that's frankly a little weird, but I love Sam so I don't say anything, especially when she points the camera down and takes a picture of all of our shoes. Felicia's are cute (she has a million cute pairs of shoes). Montana's look new, but they are just normal sneakers. Mine have a hole in the toe.

We spend the rest of the ride scanning the

water for sharks (or dolphins or whales). I swear, I can't have been mistaken. It was a shiny grey dorsal fin and I'm sure it was much too large to belong to a sweet little dolphin. What else could it have been? I may never swim again. I mean, obviously I'll swim again, but I'll make someone else swim with me. An adult. A big adult. If I swim with just Sam and Montana and Felicia then the shark would eat me for sure because I'm the biggest. I look the most like a meal.

It's really not fair.

Unless, of course, it *was* a dolphin. Just some unnaturally large dolphin who is probably bigger than all the other dolphins and on his own because he's tired of being teased. If that was the case, I'd want to swim with it for sure. Dolphins don't eat people. They just like to play. Also, he'd recognize that I was much bigger than the other kids and we'd have a special friendship. Like Flipper on that old TV show that's on late at night! I'd rather it was a dolphin than a shark, that's for sure, but my brain tells me it was almost certainly a killer shark and not something fun and playful.

We round the last island, going through a place between the islands called Porlier Pass, which "runs" really fast sometimes, like a river. It's not a river, it's the ocean, but this is what the ocean does when it's trapped in a channel between two islands and the tide goes up and down. I'm not sure I understand it myself, so you'll just have to take my word for it. I don't have time to try to explain properly even if I knew what I was talking about. Which I don't.

This time, the water is pretty still but there are swirling whirlpools. Believe you me, you don't want to fall in there. I put my hand on Montana's arm just because. I mean, I know she's not going to jump out or anything, but if she did, it would be awful. She smiles at me as if to say, "What are you doing?" And I smile back to say, "Who, me? Nothing. No, I don't think you are going to fall overboard. But I'm ever so slightly worried because bad things seem to happen to you when you're around me."

You know, there are very large octopuses (octopi?) down there. I even saw a show on the Discovery Channel about them. They're *huge.* They're as big as the living room at home. You wouldn't want to go swimming with them, no sir-ree. Although, come to think of it, you never read news stories about people being eaten by octo-puses. Or see terrifying octopus movies. There are lots of shark stories, though. It makes more sense to be afraid of sharks. Last year I read one where a shark bit off some kid's leg and his uncle jumped into the water and grabbed the leg out of the shark's mouth and drove the kid and the leg to the hospital. They sewed it back on! That's something, I'm telling you.

.What greets us around the corner is not what we were expecting at all. The entire whole trip it has been flat calm, but the Georgia Strait, which is the last bit, is, well, *roaring*. It's like a long expanse of open water and the wind sometimes howls through.

Which is when Dad says, "Oh no! It's *roaring*." For my whole life, I've been hearing people say only one of two things about this part of the water. It's either "roaring" or "flat as a baby's bum." And baby's bums aren't flat, so what does that even mean? Ridiculous. "We'll have to go into the bay," he finishes.

Which is the worst thing of all because it means a longish walk through the woods instead of a shortish walk up the hill. "Oh no!" I say. "Not the bay!"

"No huge rush," says Dad. "We can take our time."

I roll my eyes. Like doing it slowly will make it better? I don't think so.

"I don't mind, Mr. Fitz," says Montana. I glare at her. Honestly, she's just too enthusiastic about work.

The boat bucks and rolls like a horse (not that I'd know as I don't ride horses, but I'd like to. Everyone else does. Montana does, anyway. Only

Mum says I already take too many lessons and that I don't have any time). Dad slows the engine down to a crawl. It's so beautiful and sunny and hot and it seems so wrong that the waves are so huge. Felicia looks a bit green.

"I hate this part," she says.

"Me too," says Sam.

Blue barks in agreement. I mean, what's to like? Everyone hates this bit. We go super slowly and finally get into the bay and unload everything onto the beach, which is also blazing hot. There is something about this bay, which is my favourite, in that it seems to always be about a million degrees hotter than everywhere else. I take a big deep breath and I can smell the ocean and the rotting seaweed and something gross and the nice, fresh, green smell of the trees and nettles and shrubs and moss and stuff.

Blue barks and runs around in circles and plunges into the water and starts swimming.

"Come back, Blue!" I shout, and he does, which is good because even though it's hot, we don't have time to swim. We have a lot of carrying-stuff-to-the-cabin to do. Slowly. Or whatever.

I notice that Sam is clicking pictures like crazy. She's a little ways down the beach when suddenly she shouts, "Gross!"

So naturally we all go running to look. When we climb over a heap of logs, we all gasp with horror.

Because what we see is a big rotting carcass of a dead seal. Blue gets super excited and immediately jumps into it, like it's a hot bath full of nice-smelling bubbles.

"BLUE!" Dad shouts and pulls him out. The stink is overwhelmingly, horrifyingly bad. I mean it. It's about the grossest thing I've ever smelled in my entire life.

Montana gags. "I'm going to be sick!" she says.

We all run as far away from it as we can, giggling and also grossed out and all sort of gagging because when one person does, it's like everyone else has to. I throw up a tiny bit in my mouth, which is very very horrible, I don't mind telling you.

"I wonder what killed it?" I say after I spit on the rock to try to get the taste out. "Maybe it was a shark!"

"Maybe," says Sam. "Maybe it was the same shark that you saw!"

"I don't know if I want to swim here," says Felicia, looking dubiously at the water in the bay, which is clear and dark green and, frankly, very inviting. A drib of sweat trickles down my nose.

"Sharks don't come into bays," I say quickly, like I know this sort of thing. As soon as I say it, I totally believe it myself.

"Oh," she says. "Still . . . "

We don't have too much time to debate it

because we have to start taking loads of stuff to the cabin. We pile bunches of it into wheelbarrows, which people leave there for other people to use, and start pushing through the woods, which is harder than it sounds. I'm just about to say, "Watch out for the nettle!" when Felicia yells, "Ouch!"

I feel terrible that she got nettled. It's probably my fault for not reminding her. I mean, it's no fun to be lumpy and itchy, which she is, as I'm sure you can imagine.

As we get closer to the cabin, my heart starts beating a good bit harder, both from excitement and from the fact that my wheelbarrow has all the food in it and weighs about two tons. Seriously, my legs and shoulders are killing me. Why did I have to get the heaviest one?

I don't complain, though. Remember, I'm trying to be nicer.

Basically the second we can see the cabin, we just look at each other and park the wheelbarrows all in a row. Boy oh boy, I love this cabin. It's not like the most beautiful building in the world, but it's The Cabin. I mean, it's just the greatest place. My eyes kind of well up for no reason, which I have to try to hide by coughing like crazy. Montana pats me on the back like I'm randomly choking on something and then she gives me a hug, because she's a nice person and I guess she figures that I'm sad for mysterious reasons.

I *am* sad for mysterious reasons, but that's beside the point. I shake her off a bit. I mean, sometimes her niceness is buggy. We all just stand there for a few seconds and stare at stuff, like the water barrels and a tree that's fallen over on the front path. Dad is behind us still, in the woods. The cabin looks funny because all the windows are covered with plastic or wood to protect them from winter storms and there are extra pieces of wood over all the doors. It's so sealed up, it's not like we can go in and start unloading stuff, right?

So what we do instead, without really saying anything, is to run straight down the hill to the beach, shedding our sweatshirts as we go. It's really hot and it finally feels like Real Summer has begun! Yippee! We all start sort of laughing and shouting, which is funny, so we laugh harder.

The waves are crashing against the shore, which is all sandstone, and leaving a trail of white foam on the rocks. The tide is super-duper low so we can see our favourite tide pools all just lying out there in the sun waiting to be explored and whatnot. Everyone wants to do everything at once, like fish in the tide pools for minnows and look under rocks for eels and go for a walk to see if there are bats in the cave that's halfway down the beach and look through the logs for treasures like glass floats from Japanese fishing boats.

"Let's look for gold!" says Sam.

"Nah," says Felicia. "We looked last winter and it's not here. That was *last* time. *This* time, let's do something different!"

"But we're the Gold Diggers Club!" says Sam, looking kind of disappointed.

"We can look for gold maybe later," I say, to be nice. Not that I want to look for gold again, because I'm pretty sure it isn't here. I think it was just a story made up to make people think there was gold when there wasn't. Besides, I just want to play. Even thinking the word "play" makes me cringe a little bit. What if we are too old to "play" now? I mean, if I say "play," will they think I'm kind of a little kid still? Also, why am I worried about this in front of my very best friends?

"I wish we could swim," I say. "I'm so hot."

"But what about the sharks?" says Montana.

"There aren't any here," I say confidently, even though I'm not confident. Anyway, we can't swim here, we'd have to walk back down to the bay. It's too rough out in front of the cabin off the unprotected shore. The waves are rollers. So instead of doing anything, we just plop down on the rocks. The rocks are amazing because they suck up all the heat from the sun, like big sponges, only they aren't soft. It's like sitting down on a warm electric blanket, but it's a rough, scratchy rock and you're at the beach.

"I wonder if your dad needs help," says Montana. See? She can't stop being helpful, even if no one needs help.

I shrug, a little bit madly. I mean, I don't *want* to help, I want to just sit here and be a kid. "I don't know," I say. "I'm sure he'll come down here and yell at us if he does."

"How are we going to put in the mooring?" asks Sam. Sam is very goal-oriented.

"It's too rough," I say wisely, eyeing the waves like I know what I'm talking about.

"I know," she says, "But I still want to know how it's done."

I sigh. "Well, first there is a big block of cement we build at the lowest of the low tide lines. And then we attach it to the dinghy. Then we wait until high tide and we drag it out and sink it down with the chain attached. Then we put the floaty thing on the top." To be honest, I've forgotten the actual order that this happens in. Is it high tide or low tide?

"Oh," she says. "Cool."

Of course, just then Dad appears with the wheelbarrow full of concrete mix and says, "Get to work!"

"Ugh," I say. "We just sat down!" But the other girls do it like they are never happier than when they are doing chores. I'm not so sure they're like this around their own dads, but whatever. I get up to drag my feet and follow them, when I notice something in the waves.

"Wait!" I yell. I try to get closer to it, but the rocks are really slippery where the waves are crashing up on the beach.

"What is it?" says Sam. She's taking pictures, of course. Of everything. The problem with digital cameras is that you can take a hundred million pictures without running out, like you would on an old-fashioned camera, so there is no real reason for her not to, except that it's annoying. And that I'm sure my hair is all plastered down on my head in a non-picture-worthy way.

But that's not what I'm worrying about right then. Not really. Because right there in the waves, is the big grey body of . . .

something!

But what *is* it?

"What *is* it?" echoes Felicia.

"I think it's a shark!" I say. I'm totally excited. I mean, I'm scared of sharks, but this one isn't very big and it's not every day that you get to see one.

The body of whatever it is is getting really beaten up by the waves. Dad comes closer.

"It's a porpoise!" he says.

"A porpoise!" says Montana.

"Is it dead?" says Felicia.

"I don't know," says Dad. He slips down the rocks a bit. A wave comes up and slaps him in the leg and he nearly falls over. His jeans are totally soaked. The problem with getting your jeans soaked is, of course, that they get really heavy and then if you get pulled into the water you can't swim because your legs are all heavy and then you drown.

"Don't drown, for Pete's sake!" I yell. I mean, honestly. I don't want to say anything, but I have a nagging fear of people drowning. Pretty obviously because of my Real Dad, but I don't want to talk about it. Instead, I just get all irritated with them for fooling around in the water like that.

I close my eyes and shake my head really hard to get that thought to go away. Sometimes that works. I have to do it really hard, though, and then I look funny, but so what? It works.

We all try to get closer but the rocks are as slippery as anything. Seriously, water on sandstone is a lot like oil on pavement. It's slick as an ice rink and I was never good at ice skating. I kind of slide down on my bum to get closer and a wave comes up and nearly pulls me out to sea, which would be a fine kettle of fish, as you can imagine. I just barely hold onto the land, and I'm knee-deep in very cold water.

"Argh!" I scream.

"Don't panic, Carly!" Dad yells, pulling me out.

I mean, the water wasn't very deep, it was just a little startling. And freezing, like I said.

Just then the porpoise makes a sort of snorting sound.

"It's alive!" yells Sam. She's staying farther up the rocks, probably so she doesn't get her camera wet.

"I think it's hurt," Dad says. "Now hold on and let's think about this."

I'm already wet, so while he's *thinking,* I get into the water and put out my hand and touch the porpoise. I don't know why I do it. I mean, I know you shouldn't touch animals in the wild, but I just get the feeling that this porpoise wants someone to touch him. "You'll be okay," I whisper.

His skin feels so neat, all smooth and wet and rubbery. I'm telling you, if you ever get a chance to touch a porpoise, like if you're in a place where porpoise touching is allowed, you should touch one.

"We'll need ropes," says Dad suddenly.

"Oh!" says Montana. "Then we can make a pulley and pull him out!"

"Right," says Dad. "But what we really want to do is just pull him out of the waves and into a more protected bit of water so we can see if he's hurt."

We all get up and look around. A small distance away, there is a little bit of a rocky point, which makes a small kind of bay that isn't really a bay, but there aren't any waves actually crashing there and trying to smash people (or porpoises) into smithereens. It's more of a gentle nudging. My dad peels off his wet jeans. Luckily, he's wearing his swimming trunks underneath. Thank goodness. And Felicia runs all the way up to the dinghy that's stored under a tree partway up the hill and pulls out a big roll of rope. I don't know where it came from, honestly, but it's very convenient that it's there. I help Dad wrap the rope around the porpoise and then he plunges into the waves and kind of drags the porpoise with him.

I'm a little scared, to tell you the honest to goodness truth, because the waves are big and I know that it's hard to swim in waves like that, much less pulling a porpoise — who is probably pretty scared himself — behind you. But somehow, he does it. We all scramble after him along the shore, trying not to slip on the super-slippery rock. Well, no one else slips, but I do, on the wet green seaweed, and I skin my knee on a big fat clump of barnacles, which hurts a good bit but pales in comparison to the excitement of touching a porpoise, I can tell you that. I mean, that's a once in a lifetime experience and I already have a trillion barnacle scars so one more won't make any difference.

Finally, after forever, Dad emerges from the water. The porpoise is kind of bobbing around and looking at us with his big black eyes. He's so cute,

I can't stand it. I totally want to keep him forever, like Flipper (who is on that old TV show, like I mentioned before), but I know that's not *real*. Also, this porpoise is hurt and probably terrified out of his wits. Dad is still standing in the water with him, and he's kind of looking him over. It's not like he's a vet or anything so I don't know how he knows what to look for or what. Sam is taking pictures like crazy and Montana is nearly falling in the water trying to see what Dad is seeing.

"He's been shot!" Dad says, finally.

"What?" we all say at the same time. I mean, that's seriously shocking. Who would shoot a porpoise? I can't imagine anyone who would do that. And why?

Dad points to a spot on the porpoise's back, right behind the dorsal fin, that looks like a black mark. "I'm pretty sure it's a bullet hole," he says.

"Goodness," says Felicia. "I wonder if that's what happened to that seal."

"I wonder," says Dad, frowning. "Why would someone do that?"

I kind of reach down to pat the porpoise. Everyone knows that porpoises are just as smart as people, if not smarter, and if he's really smart he probably knows he's been shot and it probably hurts.

"Hmm," says Dad, hoisting himself up out of the water. "I'm going to go get the phone and make some calls. You girls keep an eye on our friend here."

"Okay," we all say. Like you'd be able to drag us away. A real live porpoise! On our beach! It takes us about two seconds to all get into the water with him. We don't want him to feel lonely. Or scared, so we try to be really gentle.

Just then, the porpoise kind of makes a funny chirping sound, which is about the coolest thing I've ever heard and also very startling.

"Let's give him a name!" says Sam.

"Good idea," I say. I consider myself a naming expert, to tell you the truth. I think about names a lot. Apparently, there is a religion you can join, like a club, where you get to choose your own name so that it suits you. This sounds A-okay to me, although I don't know about the religion part, but as far as I'm concerned, maybe when you turn eighteen or something, you should get to pick what you want to be called. I sure wouldn't pick Carly, I don't think. I think I'd pick something pretty and unusual, like Skye-with-an-*e*. That's pretty.

"We could call him Skye!" I say, because I love the name and obviously I'm stuck with Carly.

"But that's a girl's name," says Sam.

"I like it," says Montana.

"We don't know that it's not a girl," says Felicia. "I mean, how can you tell?"

"I don't know," frowns Sam. "He just looks like a boy. I think we should call him Jack."

"Jack!" says Montana. "I like that."

"You like everything," I say, not to be mean, but because I liked it better when she liked the name I chose. "We should vote," I say.

So we vote and two people (Montana and Sam) vote for Jack, and me and Felicia vote for Skye. I feel myself starting to get upset. I mean, it's my cabin, so really it's my beach and my porpoise. I shoot a glare at Montana, but then I make myself try to look as close to the sun as I can, which actually hurts my eyes a lot. I don't recommend it. Huh — I was just trying to stop the madness from getting away on me. Now I have a bigger problem to contend with, which is really sore eyes.

"Um," she says. "Maybe we could use both names?"

"What do you mean?" says Sam.

"Like, we could call him/her Skye Jack or Jack Skye," she says.

"I like Jack Skye!" says Felicia.

"We could vote again," I say dubiously.

"No!" says Montana. "Jack Skye is fine."

"I like Skye Jack," I say, just to disagree. Then I see that she looks maybe like she might cry. I don't want to have a fight about it, it's really not worth it. So we all stand with our hands on the porpoise's back and say, "We christen thee Jack

Skye!" Just then Dad comes running down the hill.

"I called the animal rescue centre," he says. "They're going to send a boat." Also, he's brought sandwiches that Jenny packed in the cooler. We sit on the beach and have a picnic and Jack Skye bobs around in the water and I imagine that he's thinking, "Gee, I wish I had a sandwich because I'm a good bit hungry," so I throw mine into the water, but he doesn't eat it. Then I kind of wish that I hadn't because, well, I'm awfully hungry, too.

It seems like no time at all has passed, even though it's been a couple of hours. The skin on my legs is starting to turn pink, but I don't want to go get sunscreen and put it on in case I miss something that Jack Skye does. What, I don't know, because he really just bobs around in the tide, but you know what I mean. Every once in a while he does make a sound, which is really neat and cool. Anyway, we're all just sitting there chatting and taking pictures of Jack Skye and pretending that he's ours to keep, when a big boat comes around the point. It says *Wild Animal Rescue* on the side in big letters. To tell you the honest to Pete truth, it reminds me a little bit of when Montana had to be rescued after her back accidentally got broken when we were diving off the rock last summer, and I feel my heart speed up a good amount, like

I'm scared, even though I'm not.

A bunch of people get off the boat and come to shore in a Zodiac, which is neat. I'd like to have a Zodiac, which is a rubber boat with a big engine that goes really fast. They are all taking about Jack Skye and looking him over and having a serious conversation with Dad about where we found him and stuff and no one really talks to us and we're kind of pushed out of the way. Next thing we know, Jack Skye is being hoisted up by this lifty thing onto the big boat and they disappear around the point, and we're just left there on the beach all talking at once.

"What did they say?"

"Is Jack Skye going to be okay?"

"Where are they taking him?"

"What's going to happen?"

And Dad kind of holds up his hands and laughs and says, "One at a time! I can't answer all your questions, but they're going to take him to the Aquarium where they can look after him until he's better and they're launching an investigation with the police into who's shooting the animals. They might come back to look at the dead seal to see if there's a bullet hole in him, too."

"Oooh," says Sam. "It's like a mystery."

"Hmmm," says Dad, frowning at me. "Now don't get any funny ideas in your head, Carly. I'm sure the police can look after this."

"Right!" I say cheerfully, but secretly I'm already imagining the four of us cracking the case and maybe even getting our pictures in the newspaper. I wink at my friends and they wink back, and right away I know that we're all thinking the same thing.

That's how best friends do things, you know. Sometimes we don't even have to talk about it.

chapter 5

So, I should tell you that with all the excitement of Jack Skye — which was probably the most interesting and neat thing to ever happen to me — and the fact that the strait was "roaring" all day on Saturday and Sunday, we didn't get the mooring done at all because of all the technical whatever about the tide and whatnot. Which is too bad. Dad says that was the "best" tide of the year and it has to be super-low and also super-high to make the mooring block easy to move. I never can quite get it straight. In any event, we didn't mind so much not doing the mooring because that gave us lots of time to explore and make a new trail and build a fort in the woods. Also, we had a big beach fire and roasted marshmallows and hot dogs. I don't even really like hot dogs but I certainly do if I've roasted them myself. I can't explain. They just taste better.

I know Dad feels terrible about the mooring,

like he abandoned Mum (who was fine without us anyway) and then didn't do the main thing he wanted to do. I know he'll do it sometime during the week on a day trip with some friend of his, but still he fretted all the way home. The really weird thing is that Mum cried like mad when we called her from the boat and she heard we didn't even do the mooring. Then she cried more when we told her about Jack Skye. Dad says it's the "baby blues." She cries more than she used to (well, she never really used to cry at all) and none of her clothes fit. Oh, and of course she has a wailing baby on her at all times.

Poor old thing. I never thought I'd feel sorry for Mum because she's always been like this super-strong not-feeling-sorry-for person. Now she's a mess. The baby blues. Huh. Another reason why living in an apartment by yourself when you grow up sounds good.

I wonder what Jack Skye is doing right now. I hope he's okay. My legs are a tiny bit red and sore and itchy from being sunburned, so I reach down and scratch them vigorously with my ruler, which leaves interesting white lines all over them. I'm just inspecting these scratches when I hear the teacher clear his throat as though he's swallowed a bullfrog. It's quite gross.

I should explain that instead of being outside or enjoying my life even the teensiest amount, I'm sitting in a classroom with a bunch of other dunces in Summer Math "Camp." Which is most definitely *not* a camp of any variety. I smile at the teacher as angelically as possible. It would be no good having him hate me so early in the class.

Overall, the whole thing is basically my worst nightmare. Outside, it's all sunny and there are kids who don't have to be trapped in a stifling hot school (not even MY school, some other ugly purple school a million miles away that I have to get driven to because it's too far to walk) who are playing outside and laughing and screeching to beat the band. Really, could they be having *that* much fun? Huh. To make it worse, just a few minutes ago, I saw the ice cream truck go by.

It's *totally* unfair. That's all there is to it. I'm trying to listen to this totally irritating teacher, who is a very tiny man with a grating accent. (I used to like English accents but now I don't.) He wears a bow tie (what is it with teachers and bow ties?) and right now he's going on and on and on and on about triangles, but I can't concentrate. Instead, I'm drawing a picture of Jack Skye in my notebook. I'm thinking that when I get home, I can get a proper picture on the computer and make iron-on things for sweatshirts. I have this idea that every time I have an adventure that's unusually excellent with my friends, I'll make them a shirt to celebrate. It is also handy that dolphins are the mascot of my diving club because then I can wear it for both. I'm thinking of getting hoodies, which are cooler than regular sweatshirts because of the hoods. But who will pay for them?

Forget it. I don't have any money. What was I thinking? I can't be giving away sweatshirts every six seconds anyway. Basically, if we got sweatshirts, I'd have to get an XXL so that I'd never grow out of it.

I hate being too tall for my clothes. I swear, my arms are like the arms of a monkey. I kind of hold them up to see how long they are and the teacher says, "Yes . . . Carly, is it?"

And I realize that he thinks I was asking a question and I don't even know what he was talking about, so I blush and say, "Sorry, I was stretching."

"Hmm," he says, like he's already got me black-listed. He writes something down in his notebook. Great. Maybe he's taking notes on our behaviour and he'll fail me out of Summer Math Torture because I stretched *accidentally*. Sheesh. Is there a rule about *stretching* now? I mean, please. Give me a break.

Then I hear someone snickering in the back — like really snickering; he sounds like a horse — so I turn around to see who it is (most kids in here are kids I've never seen before) and it's Nigel. Why is *he* in remedial math? I thought he was all super-math smart-person, or at least that's what he led everyone to believe in the five whole days he was enrolled in my class. How could he have had time to fail regular math when he's only been in school for a week of museum outings and beach picnics? He claimed to be some sort of prize-winning math whiz! He lied!

Hmmph.

I glare at him and he grins at me, like he's the funniest person to ever walk the earth. Well, he's not. I write his name in my notebook and then draw big lines through it. Ugh.

"Oh, Nigel," says the teacher. "I didn't hear you come in."

"I've been here the whole time, Uncle Matt," he says.

Uncle Matt?

Uncle Matt?

Could my life get any worse?

Yes, it could.

"Oh, I didn't see you!" says the teacher, laughing like mad. I can see that strange laugh styles run in their family. "Class, I'd like you to meet my nephew Nigel, who is going to be your peer tutor. He's just brilliant at Maths and he just moved here from England."

Am I dreaming? Am I having a horrible nightmare? I swear that I actually see spots drifting in front of my eyes, so much that I have to put my head between my knees. I contemplate throwing up. As I dangle my head towards the floor, I notice that I have chewed gum on my shoe, which I pick off with my pencil. Gross. By the time I've done this, the teacher has moved on to other things. I decide that the only way to handle this horror show is to just completely ignore Nigel. I give my head a shake to firm up this decision. Ignored! I've erased him. He doesn't exist.

I have more important things to dwell on anyway. For example, after math class today I've got two hours of diving, and then I'll *finally* get to go home and see Mum and Nicholas Zane, the little BaaBaa. I can hardly remember what he looks like, it seems so long since I've seen him. I should explain that we got home from the cabin really late and I stayed the night with Sam as a "special treat" (which means that Mum thought I'd be too much to bother dealing with, seeing as she now has the baby to worry about). Dad said it was because the baby would likely keep me awake at our house. Ha. Like I can't see through that lame excuse.

Anyway, Sam and I stayed up all night talking about Jack Skye. We sort of were pretending that because we found him, and he was shot, we'd somehow get to keep him and he'd hang around the docks waiting for us all the time. We also talked about how, because we found him, it was probably our job to find out who did this to him and why. Like we'd be detectives, sort of. Animal Detectives, like that show on the Animal Channel on TV.

The truth is that we're not entirely sure how to go about being detectives. The only thing I know about detecting is what I read in these old books of Mum's called Nancy Drew. There were about a million books and they were all yellow. Anyway, Nancy always seemed to have access to things, like knowing what kind of bullet it was, which would lead her right back to the perp. *Perp* is a word that is short for something and means "bad guy." I like using the word *perp* because it makes me sound much more like I know what I'm doing, which I don't. Nancy Drew always did her detective work wearing matchy-matchy sweaters and skirts and often pearls around her neck. That would be such a nuisance, if you ask me. I'd rather do detective work in shorts and a hoodie sweatshirt with a picture of a dolphin on it (which I can't afford to buy).

I yawn and stretch again. Oh no! Right away I look at Mr. Whatsit to see if I've accidentally done something bad *again.* But luckily, he isn't looking at me. Instead, he's writing something on the overhead projector. A pop quiz! In summer school? That's crazy! It's delusional! It's tragedic!

I kind of panic and break my pencil on the

paper trying to write all the stuff down, so I have to go to the back to sharpen it. Of course, when I'm hurrying back there, I trip right over Nigel's ugly foot. I swear, he stuck it out on purpose and was only pretending to stretch at the same time. I don't know what this boy's problem is. It seems that his whole entire purpose in life is to torture me and make me feel stupid. I try to think of something I can do in return, but I can't think of anything, so I just knock his book off his desk on my way by and smile sweetly and say, "Oh, excuse me," and he laughs like it's funny, which it most certainly is not. It was meant to be mean.

The quiz is completely impossible and I barely have time to finish it or to think about anything else, when I look out the window and see Dad's car parked there to take me to diving practice. This dumb math class sure went by quickly. I throw my quiz on Nigel's Uncle Matt's desk and run out of the building. It's so summery outside, it makes me want to cry and to laugh. It's summer! Yay!

I don't have much time to celebrate that, though, because it's off to Summer Diving Camp. Another camp! That isn't a camp. Why is everything called "camp"? It shouldn't be called "camp" unless there is over-nighting involved and canoes and classes where they teach you how to make a wallet out of a piece of leather and a bone needle, in my opinion. But whatever. Dolphin Diving *Camp*, it is.

"How was math?" Dad says.

I just shrug.

"Is there anyone you know in the class?" he says.

"Why?" I say. There is no one I know in the class, except Nigel, of course, and no one else was particularly friendly, not that I care. I mean, I have lots of friends.

"Just curious," he says.

"Just this stupid boy named Nigel," I tell him. "He's from England."

"Oh," says Dad. "He probably has to take it because the lessons are taught differently there or something. Isn't that interesting?"

"Not really," I say as rudely as possible. "Besides, he's some math freak genius. He just has no friends and nothing else to do so he's helping out. Not that I care." Frankly, the last thing I want to talk about is Nigel and/or math. It's summer! Math pollutes summer with its mathness! Nigel pollutes everything with his Nigelness!

"How's the baby?" I say. I should mention that Dad is off work for a few weeks to "help" Mum with the baby. I'm guessing he isn't that much help. He sort of gets lame and helpless around the baby, from what I've seen. He's like, "What do I do?"

"Noisy!" says Dad, and then he laughs. "But he sleeps a lot during the day."

That's just backwards, if you ask me. I mean, wouldn't it be better if he cried all day and then slept all night? If he were my baby, I'd keep him awake all day and if I saw him drifting off, I'd wake him up. Anything to make him sleep at night.

"So . . . " Dad says. It looks like he's struggling for something to say. "Um, are you excited about diving?" he says.

"Sure," I say, shrugging so I look like I don't care. The actual total truth is that I'm very excited, even though it's the same coach and the same kids I dive with all the time. There's something about the fact that it's every weekday for two hours that makes it seem different and more exciting and more professional than regular diving classes. It's sort of like a job, only I'm not dumb enough to think you do a job for only two hours a day unless you're lucky and you're a movie star or something like that.

Suddenly, Jack Skye pops into my head again. "Did you hear from the police about the type of bullet used to shoot Jack Skye?" I say. I take my notebook out in case I have to write anything — otherwise I'll forget important information. Mum says I'm very "scatterbrained" and I don't want to let Jack Skye down.

"What do you have there?" says Dad, nearly

driving off the road to see. I mean, he really likes to know *everything.* "I haven't heard anything yet, by the way. I don't really expect to."

"Nothing," I say, trying to smile mysteriously and to write down what he said, which is hard to do in a moving vehicle. "I haven't heard anything yet" is not much of a clue. Even I know that. Maybe this whole detective idea is just lame. I stuff the notebook into my backpack because we're pulling up at the pool, and I grab my other backpack with my suit and stuff in it and race inside without even waiting for a goodbye from Dad.

I don't mind telling you that there is no smell in the world better than the chlorine-y smell of pools and there is no sound better than the echo-y sound of pools. Boy oh boy, I love pools.

I change quickly and cram my stuff into a locker. When I get out to the pool, I'm pretty surprised to notice Dad in the stands watching. It makes me feel a tad bit nervous, but I always feel a little nervous when I'm diving anyway — but not in a bad way, in a good way, like you always want to feel a little bit nervous because it keeps you from making dumb mistakes, which I make anyway but that's not the point. Jon says the funny nervous-but-not-nervous feeling is adrenalin. Whatever it is, it's good, but also bad. Well, you have to try it to know what I mean.

Because it's the first day of "camp" we all have to introduce ourselves to each other, which is hilarious because we all know each other already. We've all been diving together forever. I spot Sam running in (late) finally. She nearly falls all over herself laughing about how she almost tripped.

"Carly and Sam," says Jon in his I-mean-business voice. "If you two can't behave your-selves properly and take this seriously, you can spend the whole class swimming laps."

Ugh! No thanks.

I mean, I love swimming but I'd rather dive, so I zip my lip closed with my finger so that he knows that I know what he's saying and that I am paying attention.

"Blah blah blah," he says. "Diving goals and blah blah blah and drills blah blah blah." I'm sure it was very interesting, but I couldn't hear very well. I must have got water in my ears from the shower on the way in. I hate when that happens. To get it out, I hop up and down on one leg, then another, and I fall over. Pool decks are almost always slippery. I wonder why they don't make them all out of that rubbery stuff so kids aren't always falling over.

"Carly!" he yells.

Honest to Pete, sometimes I feel like people are always yelling at me for no really good reason. I'm sure other people hop up and down on one foot when they have water in their ears. Why is it a crime when I do it? It's like stretching in math class. Forget about it.

Right away, Jon breaks us up into groups to do drills. Drills don't sound like fun, but they are. They're sort of like diving without the fancy stuff, like we go up and do our thing, but we dive without doing the twist or whatever. It's like doing half-versions of real dives. In one, we see how high up we can go off the springboard, and the other, we see how much we can point our toes. I realize it doesn't sound fun. You have to love diving to love it.

After the first hour, he splits us up again and half of us go to work with Cassie, who is like a ballerina. She teaches us stretches and ballet stuff which is supposed to make us more supple, which means loose. Also, we have to lift weights. The rest of the class gets to do proper dives, which makes me mad, because even though I love Cassie, I'd rather dive. Sam is in the other group. Why is he splitting us up?

Finally, after what was probably the most gruelling workout of all time, it's time to change and shower and go home. When I come out, Dad says, "You looked really good out there, Carly!" And I can tell he's trying to be really supportive and stuff, which is nice. He reads parenting books all the time and they tell him things like, Pretend to care what your kid or your step-kid is doing! So I know he's doing it because he read it in a book, but still it's nice that someone cares.

We stop on the way home and get a big bucket of fried chicken and potato salad, which is my favourite summer food. I'm kind of excited to see the baby because I haven't seen him in three days! Maybe he'll have changed or whatever, or maybe Mum will be different and more relaxed and happy.

We pull up to the house and Roo nearly falls over herself trying to run down the stairs to greet me. If no one else in this family cares if I'm alive or not, I know that Roo always does because she gets so excited that sometimes she accidentally pees. I realize this doesn't sound flattering, but it is. It's a compliment in dog-ville. Trust me.

I run into the house and Mum says, "Shhh!" She looks all frantic and harried, just like before, and I'm a bit bummed out, but then she points and I can see that the baby is sound asleep. He looks so sweet, just like a little doll. I kind of want to pick him up and hug him and squish him. Not really squish him, but like in a hug. You know what I mean.

Mum whispers, "How was practice?"

And I whisper back, "It was good!"

And she whispers, "I have a surprise for you!"

And I whisper, "What is it?"

But she's already leading the way downstairs, and when we get there I just about burst into tears.

But not because I'm sad, but because I'm so *happy*. I guess when we were away for the weekend, Grandma and Aunt Lucy came over to help her fix up my new room. And there it is, *exactly* as I wanted it last year, with chocolate brown carpet *and* light purple walls and there is even one of those canopy things over the bed with mosquito netting that look so pretty, like a princess's veil. I get a little choked up and I yell, "Thank you!" I hug her really hard. Which is weird, because her belly feels really strange and soft. I'm used to hugging her with her big hard belly getting in the way. This was a bit like hugging a pudding-filled pillow, if you must know the truth.

"Ew!" I say, without meaning to.

"I know," she says sadly and pats her stomach. "But it will go away fast once I start exercising again!"

"Of course it will," I say supportively, even though I secretly can't imagine it. Also, what happens to all the extra skin? But I don't think about that too much because I'm too excited just to sit on my bed in my new room and look around at the walls and stuff and to get onto my computer (which is on my new desk!) and start sending email to my friends so that they can hear all about my room. I'm sure they'll be very excited. I'm just about to turn on the computer when I hear a *knock knock knock* on the door and it's Dad and he has a big wrapped something in his hand.

"It's not my birthday!" I tell him. Like maybe he got mixed up and I don't want him to be embarrassed if he got it wrong.

"I know!" he says. "But I got you a New-Room Present."

"Goody!" I say. I don't even bother to pretend to be blasé, because after all, who doesn't like presents for no reason? So I rip it open and it's a big framed poster of a porpoise who looks *just* like Jack Skye, only not quite. Exactly like him, except without the bullet hole. It's just the sweetest thing I've ever seen.

"It's the sweetest thing I've ever seen!" I say. Dad helps me hang it up on the wall. I'm so excited about my new room, I don't notice at first how quiet it is down here, until Dad starts to hammer the nail in for the picture hook and I remember the baby and say, "Don't! You'll wake the baby!" (which is something that everyone in this house is going to have said a billion kajillion times before this summer is over, I'll bet) and he laughs and says, "It won't wake the baby. This room is soundproofed!"

Soundproofed!

"Soundproofed!" I shout, because I can.

It is just too good to be true. I just have to lie down on my new bed, it's so good, and pull the veil-bed-canopy thingamajig closed around me so I can cry a little bit. I don't know what's wrong with me lately, but sometimes I just feel like crying more than a little bit. I want to cry a good amount. It's weird and I can't explain it, so don't ask me to.

"Come up for dinner when you're ready," he says cheerfully, and I can tell he's pretending to not know that I'm crying, which makes me cry a little bit more that he would be so nice to me, and he's not even my Real Dad. Which gets me thinking about my Real Dad, which makes me cry even more because he died. Right on my new bedside table, there is a picture of him in his Greek fisherman's cap, which he wore all the time, and he's on the boat and it's obviously windy because his face is squinched up in that look that people get when wind is blowing in their eyes. I just miss him a lot, and I give up and cry really really super hard for about five minutes, and then I feel better and I go upstairs for chicken.

There isn't too much that could keep me away from a big bucket of chicken, I can tell you that.

I run up the stairs and right away I can hear all the noise that I cannot hear at all in my new perfect bedroom. The baby is wailing and Marly is shouting at Shane and Dad is shouting at Marly for shouting at Shane, and I can feel myself smiling like crazy because I'm the luckiest person in the whole house that I can't hear any of this, and I'm thinking about that when I realize that if I'm in the room that was Jenny's, then where is Jenny?

"Where's Jenny?" I shout, to be heard above the screeching. Seriously, it sounds like what I would imagine it would sound like if you were trapped in a room with a bunch of those noisy parrots that everyone thinks are cute but turn out to be loud squawkers. I know this because Dad's ex-wife has one and it screeches like crazy. It's pretty and stuff, but oh boy, you wouldn't want to listen to that all the time, I can promise you.

My mum looks at me. "Jenny is going back to school," she says. "So she isn't going to live with us anymore now that her summer classes are starting. But she's going to come over during the day to help me out with stuff when she has breaks in her days. And then we'll have everything in some kind of routine and we won't need her anymore because . . . " and then she pauses. Then she says, "I'm not going back to work!"

She sounds so happy that I don't have much time to be sad about Jenny. I'll miss Jenny, but really, she wasn't family. I knew she was eventually going to go. It's not like she could have stayed here forever. Well, she could have, but why would she have wanted to? This is the noisiest house in the universe.

Huh.

It seems a little bit wrong, to tell you the honest truth, to think of my mum at home all the time and not at work being all brisk and efficient and wearing high heels. I guess she won't have to wear those anymore. She'll be here all the time? I guess that's nice. It's weird. I don't know what to think.

I take the baby from my mum like I know exactly what to do and tell her to sit down and have some chicken, and I kind of rock him back and forth a bit and you know what? He stops crying. It's like magic. I look down into his little red face and I realize that he's kind of cute. Little Nicholas Zane. Oh boy. What a cutie pie he is. "Hi, brother," I whisper and I kiss him on the forehead. He stinks a bit like baby barf, but no one's perfect, right? Least of all me.

Not that I smell like barf. I don't. I hardly ever throw up.

I give Nicholas back to Mum when he starts to baaa again. Then I plop myself down to have my yummy dinner and to tell everyone all about Jack Skye, even though Dad probably already did, and about math class and about diving club. Really, there's sometimes just a lot to say, you know?

chapter 6

I am very disappointed to report that none of my friends could come to the cabin with me this weekend. It doesn't make any sense. How can we avenge Jack Skye and pursue the Bad Guys (or Bad Guy) (or Bad Women) if no one is allowed to leave their houses?

Huh.

So I'm sitting on the boat and pretending that I'm somewhere else entirely, such as on the 5-metre board at the Olympics.

I am, however, wearing a new hoodie sweatshirt with a picture of Jack Skye on the sleeve. It's the palest of pale pinks and it says *CAF* (which are obviously my initials) on it. It's very subtle. Mum says it just looks like I spelled café wrong, which I think is not very nice. I can hardly help what my initials are, can I?

It's Friday again and the week just passed in a blur of diving and more diving and more diving and a fair bit of boring and not-worth-mentioning math. I will tell you that Nigel (and his weirdo uncle) call it "maths," which is totally annoying, and he hangs around me way too much in class to "help" me. Huh. This is *not* the kind of help I need. The kind of help I need is the kind where I don't have to take stupid remedial math in the first place. Nigel is starting to get on my every last nerve. It's like he thinks we're friends, which we most certainly are not. Also, there is no reason for him to be there. Who has ever heard of volunteering to be a peer tutor? I mean, obviously he just moved here and has no friends, but still, it's just ridiculous. If he wants some math-freak friends who want to hang around with him and divide fractions or whatever he does for fun, he isn't going to find that at Summer Math Camp for Dummies. I can't even begin to talk about how terrible and awful and unspeakably horrible it is when he tries to so-called tutor me. Even thinking about it makes my face feel red. It's beyond bad. I can't stand it. I really can't.

Besides, if he's going to hang around summer school, he should just go right ahead and sign up for remedial English (English Camp!) to learn to speak properly instead of all Britishly. I used to like British words better than ours but now I've changed my mind.

Anyway, Marly and Shane and Mum and the

baby are all in the lower part of the boat and Dad and I are up on the flying bridge just watching all the islands fly by and *not* thinking about math, maths or Nigel.

So there.

It's super calm and a perfect summer day, but how excited can I be about the cabin if the rest of the girls aren't there? Furthermore, like it could get much more depressing, I know I'm going to be stuck "entertaining" Marly and Shane because Mum is nervous about taking the New Baby anywhere and doing anything. Really, I think she should relax. I bet babies are tougher than we think they are! I mean, didn't Native Canadian women have babies out in the woods and then continue with their lives? I saw the display at the museum. They just put them in leather things and left them to their own devices. It's not like they got maternity leave. I'm sure they didn't sit around the fire sewing stuff out of deer hides and cooing about how many times their baby went poo. And think about the Middle Ages. Do you think babies were getting all coddled when Vikings were storming cities and taking everyone's stuff? Seriously. Also, baby poo is pretty much all Mum talks about these days.

I shake my head hard to erase all thoughts of math and horrible Nigel and baby poo from it and try to think about diving. I love Diving Camp. It's seriously the best because it's so so so serious. It's like the rest of the year we're just fooling around and now it's for real because we get to practise for so long, every day. Sometimes I'm so tired after practice that, boy oh boy, does my whole body hurt. It's like I have a million billion pins and needles inside all my muscles except they also ache. It's terrible. But it's also good. It feels like the kind of hurting that is like an honour or something. That sounds dumb, but you know what I mean.

What's really cool about even the pain part is that we get to go see the Club physiotherapists afterwards and they stretch us all out if we're hurting and whatnot, which we are all the time. I imagine that Olympic athletes have their own physios on staff at all times. They can probably just call and say, "Come and stretch me out!" And someone will.

I flex my arm muscle and look at it. I'm getting very muscle-y, almost like a boy, which is fine. I don't mind a bit looking like a boy. I mean, there's no reason why a girl shouldn't be (and look) as strong as a boy in the first place. Why are girls supposed to be weak? That's just dumb, for Pete's sake. I show it to Dad and he smiles as if to say, "Nice muscle!" but he doesn't say anything. It's pretty nice to have quiet, to be truthful. I know he likes it because it's so noisy at home, so I don't make him talk.

I sit back and scan the water for dorsal fins, which might be either sharks or some of Jack Skye's family. It's driving me crazy that we haven't had any news of Jack Skye. What if he's dead? As soon as I think that, I have to close my eyes very tightly to get the thought out of my head. I give my head a firm shake, which helps. Of course he's not dead. He's fine, I'm sure. And it's up to me (because the girls have all deserted me) to figure out why he got shot in the first place. I scan the water with renewed determination and "fresh eyes." Grandma always says that if you have a problem, you should go to sleep and look at it with "fresh eyes" in the morning, so if you think about it, I'm really getting "fresh eyes" much more efficiently by just squeezing my eyes tightly shut.

So far, I can't see anything but a few logs and bunches of seaweed. I certainly can't see any dolphins or people shooting at them. I wish I was more smart about this sort of thing, like the Animal Detectives. I wish the girls were here, to be truthful, because I can hardly be expected to figure out who did it by myself.

I brought my metal detector and a notebook just in case I come across some clues. Secretly, I think maybe I *can* solve the mystery by myself. That will show them! I think they think that I'll wait for them to come next weekend, but maybe I don't need them. Maybe I'm just as smart without them. Hmmph.

I practise smiling because I'm starting to feel in a bit of a bad mood. Mum says that it's because I'm almost a teenager that I'm getting in bad moods more often, but I think it's because my life is getting more annoying.

"Carly," Dad says.

"Huh?" I say. "What?"

"We're here."

"Oh!" I say. "Sorry!"

It's always exciting when you get somewhere sooner than you think you will. Still, it basically takes a billion years to get everyone to shore. I can't even describe the drama of being on the boat rocking in the swell while Dad loads things into the dinghy to row to shore. Dogs are leaping everywhere and Marly and Shane are practically directly underneath my feet

"Careful of the baby!" Mum keeps saying, as though someone might accidentally pitch him over the side of the boat.

I wait on the boat for the longest because the kids are going to burst from excitement if they don't get to shore. While I'm bobbing there in the swell, I keep an eye out for porpoises from Jack Skye's family who are likely scouring the shoreline looking for him. I hope I see one and I will explain that Jack Skye is in the hospital getting fixed up and will be returned (I hope) as good as new. I will tell them like there isn't any doubt, though. They don't need to worry. If dolphins worry, that is.

I watch as Dad tries to row with the whole family dangling here and there in his way. Naturally, they get out right onto the slippery rock and right away Marly falls and hurts her nose (how is that possible?) and starts crying. Mum has to help her up, so Dad has to hold the baby and wait while the swell pushes him into the rocks. Honestly, I should have brought a video camera to film all this for that stupid TV show about funny (i.e. dumb) home videos. I could probably make a hundred billion dollars just from this trip alone. Or at least ten thousand.

Finally, Dad comes back for me and the dogs. They're very nearly going nuts so I hurry them into the dinghy. I have to hold onto Blue to stop him from just leaping out and swimming to shore, which might not have been such a bad thing — I was just worried that maybe a killer whale would happen along at that moment and think he was a seal and eat him.

Well, I know it's dumb. But you never know. These waters are obviously filled with dangerous creatures. I know for sure there are whales, I've seen them. And sharks. And dolphins.

By the time Dad and I have single-handedly dragged all the food and supplies up the hill, we are sweltering to the very death. Mum can't help because she is looking after the baby. Honestly, I wish I had a baby because then I could just walk around holding it and not doing any real work. Only not really. I wouldn't want that ugly skin-bag stomach. Or the sleepless nights.

It takes forever to get dinner ready and then we all collapse into bed. I have the best sleep ever. There is something about sleeping in a sleeping bag that is just better than a regular bed, even though the sleeping bag is rustly and too hot.

In the morning I roll out of bed and everyone is up and fussing around the baby and not making breakfast. I'm starving. I've only just popped open a lukewarm lemonade (someone forgot to put them in the fridge last night) and sat down on the deck when the dogs start going all kablooey and barking and growling all over the place.

"Blue! Roo!" I call, but naturally they don't listen to me. They sound really angry and ferocious and I see the tops of two people's heads coming along the path up the hill. It's a well-worn path, even though it cuts across our property. It's *ours*, but it's used like a public path because everyone here is so friendly they don't care if people tread all over their moss. (Except some people, who do care, but that's another story.) The dogs are freaking right out and my heart starts to beat really hard in my chest. Maybe it's the Porpoise Shooters! And the dogs can sense that, which is why they sound so ferocious!

"Mum! Dad!" I yell, but it comes out as more of a croak, like your voice does in bad dreams when you think you're screaming but you find out that you can't. I don't know if this happens to you, but it's pretty much how all my nightmares go. Or those ones where you try to run and you can't. Or when all your teeth fall out and you spit them out — *pip, pip, pip* — onto the ground. They're all the same type of thing.

Anyway, Mum and Dad don't hear me because they are inside unpacking stuff, so I get up and start down the hill a bit to see who it is. I mean, I assume the dogs will protect me. Unless the strangers are Bad Guys with guns, in which case they might shoot me. But if it is the Bad Guys, I think they only want to shoot animals in the sea and I'm not an animal in the sea.

But what I see when I get close is worse than I imagined. For one thing, they aren't Bad Guys, because they are both so scared of the dogs that they're just standing there kind of frozen.

"Roo! Blue!" I call again, in my most commanding voice, and they come to me.

You see, I know it's not the Bad Guys because what it is is worse than that.

It's *Nigel*.

Think about it. What are the odds? There are

only about twenty or a hundred cabins here, spread out over miles and miles. Never in my whole life have I run into someone I know here who I didn't know *from* here, if you know what I mean.

"What are *you* doing here?" I say. I know I sound rude, but it's my island! Nigel can't be on my island! He's not allowed! He'll ruin everything.

"Hi, Carly," he says in his stupid accent. "What a fab coincidence."

"What are you *doing* here?" I say again. It's all I can say.

"I say," says the man with Nigel, "those dogs should be tied up."

"They're on their own property," I say as nastily as possible. "You're trespassing."

"You can't have vicious dogs that aren't behind a fence," he points out.

"They aren't vicious," I say. "They are trained to attack dislikable people."

"Are you a little friend of Nigel's from school?" he says.

"Yes," says Nigel at the exact moment that I say, "NO." I mean, really. We might go to the same school (for *five days*) and the same dumb remedial summer school. But we are *not* friends. He's my *tutor*. I actually don't know why I'm standing here on the hill talking to them.

"Goodbye," I say. I mean to go stomping back

up the hill without saying goodbye but it just slips out. I guess I can't help being polite.

"It was nice to meet you," says the man.

I don't say anything. I'm sure he's just as awful as his son. To tell you the truth, I'm feeling a bit upset. My Weekends at The Cabin are my favourite times in my whole *life*. Well, except for diving. And now not only are my friends not here, but the odious Nigel is going to pollute up the place with his annoyingness. I pick up my can of lemonade from the deck and go to my fort in the woods so that I can think properly. It's nice and cool and shady in there. I made it by dragging up driftwood and hammering it together to make walls. It was so long ago that the nails are rusty. It makes me a bit sad, if you want to know the truth, because my Real Dad helped me build it, a long time ago. I was really little. Probably he built the whole thing, but I remember it being "us." You know how it is.

There's a window so I can see the sea and also there is lots of salal covering the top like a roof. I push the dogs out so I can be alone and I stare at the strait, which is starting to roar. I try to look for porpoise fins, which is impossible because the waves are too big and porpoise fins are very small. It would be easier to see killer whale fins, so I look for those too.

I stare for a bit more and then I have an idea! I

write it down in my notebook. I mean, just because Nigel is in my class at school doesn't mean that he *isn't* a Bad Guy. Listen, it makes perfect sense. No animals were getting shot here last year, and he wasn't here. But this year Nigel is here and two animals have been shot. So he's obviously a prime suspect. His dad is very suspicious, too. They are obviously both very dislikable people who hate dogs. I don't trust people who hate dogs. They just seem very untrustworthy to me. Maybe in England it is okay to just randomly shoot at shiny sea creatures for sport.

Suspects, I write at the top of a new page. *Nigel*, I write. *Nigel's Dad.*

What are they doing here anyway? I hope they're just visiting someone and are never coming here again. Maybe they have a tent and the Mounties will come and tell them to leave. Or maybe — and this is a horrifical thought — they bought one of the cabins that was for sale! That would be my worst nightmare. Possibly, it would ruin my whole life.

I underline their names and lie down in the dirt and take a big slurp of my lemonade, which turns out to be a huge mistake because right away there is this terrible pain in my lip.

"ARGH!" I scream, dropping the can.

"ARGH!" I scream again, louder, because obviously no one heard (or cared) the first time. My scream clearly did not have the right degree of urgency. "HELP!" I add for good measure.

Finally my mum appears.

"What's wrong?" she says.

"MY LIP!" I scream, like it's her fault, which is probably kind of mean because it's not her fault I forgot to blow into my can to check for wasps.

"Oh, Carly!" she gasps. "I think you've been stung!"

"I know!" I say, and then — I can't help it because it hurts so much — I burst into tears.

"Oh, no," she says and hugs me. I must say, it feels like it's been a long time, like days, since she's hugged me. Also, there is a big puddle of baby barf on her shirt, which gets on my face.

"Ew!" I say and pull away. It's not that I don't want to be hugged. It's just that baby barf is gross. I don't care what anyone says.

"Let's get you some medicine," she says.

The thing is that I'm a little bit allergic to wasps. I mean, I'm not going to drop dead, but the place where I get stung swells up like crazy. Much like when I sit on a bee, but different, because it's worse and on my face. Like I don't have enough problems. Already I can see my lip even when I'm not looking. I go a bit cross-eyed and try to bring it into focus. Frankly, I'm glad I'm at the cabin and not someplace where anyone important will see me. It's only in the last week that the bee sting

I got on my bum is finally going away. Now I have a wasp sting on my face! All I need now is like a hornet sting on my stomach or something to really round this whole stinging event out.

I follow Mum inside so she can medicate me. She always has emergency sting kits at the ready, which is a very good idea and very useful. Last year Montana and I got stung by wasps after we accidentally stepped in their nest. It was awful. I have to try not to think about it so I don't cry again, when Marly comes into the cabin.

"Wha happened?" she says. She's five years old, but she still talks like a baby. It drives me crazy.

"I got stung by a wasp," I say. My voice sounds a bit funny, which is weird. I wouldn't have thought that lips had a lot to do with how your voice sounds, but apparently they do.

"Oooh," she says and she comes over and hugs my leg, which is sweet, but it kind of knocks me off balance and I fall over onto the floor.

"Don't!" I yell, because I'm startled, and she starts crying.

"Don't make your sister cry," my mum says, coming back into the room with medicine, which I swallow down while trying not to cry, myself. I can just see how this weekend is going to go, with me getting in trouble for everything that happens even when it's not my fault. Of course, at that second, the baby starts screeching like his diaper is on fire.

I grab a towel and my bathing suit. "I'm going to the beach!" I yell.

"Not by yourself!" Mum yells after me, but I pretend not to hear her. Really, I just need some time alone. Is that a crime? Besides, I'm *eleven*. It's not like anything is going to happen to me. There aren't any wild animals here to eat me and I basically know everyone on the whole island.

But still, as a compromise, I call Blue to come with me. I mean, I'm not really by myself if I have a dog, right? It's not like I'm totally disobeying.

I run through the woods, which is a weird feeling because every time I take a step and my foot hits the ground, I can feel it in my lip, which throbs. It's getting bigger by the second. I have this idea that I'll go swimming and the salt water will make it okay. Salt water is the cure for everything, in case you don't know. Like I've had a billion barnacle cuts and scrapes and they always heal up well because they happen in salt water and I guess the salt from the water goes into the cut and scrubs it out so it doesn't get all infected and gross and result in having to have your leg cut off. Not that this would happen, but it might. I saw it on TV once where this lady got a paper cut on her finger and it got infected and she suddenly, like, dropped dead. I'm not kidding. But that doesn't happen from barnacle cuts. Because of the salt water.

I'm all out of breath by the time I burst out of the forest at the beach. There are beaches all over the island but the best one for swimming is a walk through the woods away. It's the best because it's all sandy and the tide goes out really far and the bay empties out and it's all sand. But right now the tide is up about halfway so it looks like it would be about waist-deep over the sand, which is perfect for swimming. I can feel myself getting a good bit cheered up by this. I love swimming. And there are other people there that I know because I know all the island people.

"Hi, Mr. Stark!" I yell at one of them and he waves and yells, "Where are your parents?"

"They're at the cabin with the New Baby!" I shout.

"Ooh, a new baby!" one of the women says. "I must go see her! And the baby!"

"I'm going to swim," I announce.

"Good idea," someone says.

See, then I know that *they* know that I'm swimming so it's sort of like a grown-up is keeping an eye on me. I duck into someone's outhouse and change into my bathing suit, and when I come out I'm all ready to run right into the water. That's when I spot Nigel and his dad sitting with the Starks and the Hedleys. What are *they* doing here?

Naturally, I pretend not to see them. Instead, I close my eyes and plunge into the water. I guess this drives Blue a bit crazy because he leaps in after me. I'm a very good swimmer and I can swim a good amount faster than him, so I swim as fast as I can to the middle of where I know the sandbar is, where the water is warmer and also more shallow. I can still hear the people talking on the beach and I can see Nigel walking along, poking a long stick into the water, like he's going to stir it. I guess he probably doesn't swim because he's a wimp. I float on my back for a minute and let the sun warm me all up. The water is nice and warm for the top bit and under that it's freezing and also dark green. The dark green water has always spooked me a bit, to tell you the truth. I mean, I know there's nothing down there, but it looks like there could be. Like a shark.

For example.

I hold my face underwater for a minute and try to open my eyes, which hurts like crazy, so I come up spitting. I can see Nigel waving at me from the beach, so I ignore him and start doing somersaults, which is a lot of fun to do in the water. I'm pretending that I'm a porpoise, like Jack Skye, only not shot. If you've never tried it, I totally recommend it. Just remember to plug your nose or salt water goes up it and stings. This way, I figure I'm giving my sting a good bathing in the water and at the same time, I'm having fun. Doing somersaults underwater always puts me in a better mood. Even if the water is dark green and scary.

I finally come up for air and Blue is swimming smaller and smaller circles around me and Nigel is calling me.

Which is annoying.

Like I'm going to answer.

"WHAT!" I yell.

"Get out of the water!" he shouts.

"WHY?" I yell.

And he says something that I can't hear. Fine. I'm sure he's just trying to scare me by yelling "Shark!" or something, because he's obviously very much in need of entertainment, which he gets mostly by torturing me. So naturally I stick out my tongue at him and plunge back into the water to swim to the other side of the bay, i.e. as far away from him as possible.

And that's when it happens.

I can't even explain it.

It's like I dive under the water expecting it to be cool and refreshing and it's not. Then I bump into something. At first I think, "It's Jack Skye's family!" But it isn't. It's burning hot.

It's stinging! It's all over me!

I come to the surface screaming, which makes Blue swim right to me and start scratching me. I guess he thinks he is saving me, but he's hurting me.

"Ow!" I scream. The adults are all standing up and looking and Nigel is yelling, "Jellyfish!"

"Get out of the water!" they yell.

My entire body, I swear, is like completely on fire. For a second, it hurts so much I forget to be scared. I look down into the water and all around me are these big huge jellyfish with long red tentacles. We never have jellyfish at this island! I've never even *seen* one! They are seriously the size of dinner plates. Naturally, I start to cry. They're stinging my legs like crazy.

"I can't!" I yell, but it's okay because Mr. Stark is motoring towards me in his little dinghy. He just kind of plucks me out of the water and plops me in. My legs and arms and tummy are all covered with giant red welts. It stings so much I feel like I can't breathe. I can't even scream.

"Blue!" I whisper, but he is already swimming like mad to shore. I hope dogs can't get jellyfish stings.

By the time we get to shore, I am crying hysterically in a way that's too embarrassing to discuss. I must look quite a sight.

Luckily, Mr. Hedley is actually Dr. Hedley. "We need to neutralize the sting!" he says. And the adults start talking all hush-hush and I'm lying on the rock just trying to live, frankly. Like if I stop concentrating maybe the jellyfish stings will kill me. Can you die from jellyfish stings? I know you can in Australia.

"Are you okay?" says Nigel.

"Don't even talk to me," I say through gritted teeth. I'm sure he's having a good laugh at my expense. Like he probably knew the jellyfish were there when I went swimming and he wanted me to get stung. That's something a Bad Guy would do, no doubt. I give him a look that says, "I know what you're up to." And he starts freaking out and saying, "I think she's going into shock or something! Look at her face!"

"It's a wasp sting!" I croak, but no one is listening. Everyone is running all over the place.

Finally Dr. Hedley comes back and they pour something all over my legs. It feels a good bit better almost right away. And then they wrap me up in towels and, seriously, they put me in a wheelbarrow and Mr. Stark wheels me back to the cabin.

Naturally, when my mum and dad see me, they start completely freaking out. Dr. Hedley is explaining that I've been stung by jellyfish and all Mum can say is, "I told you not to go by yourself!"

Like if they'd all been there, they could have saved me? I doubt it. But I don't say anything, mostly because it hurts to talk. Or move. Or really to do anything. Whatever they poured over me stinks and it's starting to wear off.

"I think you should take her over to Gabriola," says Dr. Hedley. He means a bigger island that's near here. "They have a hospital there."

So I get wheeled down to the boat, still in my bathing suit, and Dad whisks me away before I have a chance to say anything, such as, "What did you pour all over me that stinks so bad?"

This is the worst summer of my *life*, I'm thinking as Dad zooms our boat towards the hospital. I'm sitting below deck by myself because Mum and the kids stayed at the cabin. My whole head feels swollen and my body looks like I've been attacked by a wildcat or something. All the red welts are getting huge and they hurt and itch, both, but mostly hurt. I cry a little bit, because you would too. Believe me. Anyone would.

The doctor at the hospital is really nice. He gives me a pill "for the pain," he says, which puts me directly to sleep. So I really have no idea what else he says, but I could swear he said something about pee. Weird. I fall asleep thinking about this and when I wake up again, I'm back at the cabin with white goo all over my arms and legs and the baby is crying.

Well, I think, at least I'm not dead. I mean, if you'd been stung by a wasp and a bunch of jellyfish on the same day, you'd probably be pretty relieved to be not dead, too.

I spend the rest of the weekend not talking to anyone. Mostly because it hurts to open my mouth, but also because I'm in an even worse mood than I thought possible. I look ridiculous and I still itch like crazy. Why do things that hurt at first always turn into bad itches? I don't understand it. My mum is being extra nice to me because obviously I'm ruined for life. She doesn't even make me say hi to Nigel when he hikes over from his cabin, which is about ten cabins away and over a hill from ours, to "visit" (or, more likely, torture me with his strangeness). She tells him I'm not in the mood for company and sends him away. I love my mum sometimes.

Finally, the weekend's over and I somehow survive the chaos of the trip home. Really, travelling with these people is like being in a zoo or a circus full of nut cases. As soon as I get into the kitchen, I perch myself on the stool and call the girls and tell them about my theory, that Nigel and his dad are potentially (or likely) the Porpoise Shooters. But I can tell they don't much believe me. I don't care, though, because they are all coming with us next weekend and I'll be able to prove it once and for all. I don't know how, but I will. I'm sure of it.

chapter 7

"Okay," I say, throwing myself on the bed, phone in hand. "We have to come up with A Plan!" It's Wednesday, which is the only day I have a break from Math for Dunces. Thank goodness.

"What kind of Plan?" Sam asks.

"A Plan for what?" says Montana.

I seriously love technology. I mean, we're all on the phone together, except Felicia because she's away at Violin Camp, which is a camp that actually involves sleeping overnight, unlike Diving Camp, which doesn't. Although I highly doubt there is canoeing and campfires at Violin Camp. But what do I know? It's all very confusing.

"To catch Nigel and his dad shooting the animals!" I say, tracing the pattern of jellyfish stings on my left leg with a pen. They don't hurt so much anymore as they itch and look horrible. Diving practice for the last couple of days has been some kind of embarrassing, I can tell you that much.

Everyone was pretending not to stare while they stared, and the chlorine hurt like mad. Finally Jon made me go work out with Cassie because I think he thought I was on the brink of tears, which I was, but I'm totally insulted that he thought so.

I let Treasure steal my pen. Treasure loves pens. There is no explanation for it. He rolls it off the bed and leaps after it in the most un-cat-like splat.

"Um," says Sam. "Are you sure it's them?"

"No," I say impatiently. "But they're the most obvious people and we don't have any other suspects! In detective books, the only people in the story are either Bad Guys or Good Guys and so, if you think about it, it must be them! There's no one else in the story!"

"But this isn't a story," says Montana, logically. "I mean, it's not like you saw them with guns."

"That's not the point," I say grouchily. "They are obviously Bad People."

"Didn't they save you from the jellyfish?" says Sam.

Honestly, I don't know why I'm friends with these girls if they just go ahead and doubt everything that I say. I have intuition!

"I'm being intuitioned," I say.

"You mean 'intuitive,'" says Montana.

"What," I say, "EVER."

"Don't get mad," she says.

"I'm not," I say, even though I am. I mean, we're not doing a very good job of solving this mystery. I don't say that out loud, though.

But then another thought hits me. What if Nigel and his dad maybe planted the jellyfish in the bay to sting me — you know, to get me off the trail of the case? That's what would happen if this was a weird, slightly scary movie. This perks me up immensely.

"Hey," I say, interrupting whatever it is that Sam is saying, "maybe Nigel and his dad brought the jellyfish from England or wherever, to try to steer us away from the case!"

"I don't think they have that kind of jellyfish in England," says Montana. "Besides, how could you bring a jellyfish from England?"

"I don't know," I say. "I was just thinking it would make it more like a movie if they did."

"What?" she says. But I can't explain, so I don't try. Sometimes I have thoughts that are zany even to me.

"Well," I say impatiently, "it's not like they've ever been at the island before now. I just don't like jellyfish. And I don't like Nigel."

"Right," says Montana, in a voice that sounds a little bit sarcastic, which I would think was the case if it wasn't Montana, who is never sarcastic.

"Hey, did your dad ever hear anything more

about how Jack Skye is doing?" asks Sam.

"Yes," I tell her. The truth is I forgot to tell them that Dad got a call last night from the Aquarium to say that Jack Skye had had an operation and was recovering. They thought he might be well enough to be released at the end of the summer and that his wound wasn't as bad as it looked. But that it was probably scary for him and he might be skittish and maybe won't know how to act in the wild anymore. Well, duh. Obviously it would be. No one wants to get shot, even if you are a super-smart porpoise. He'll be swimming with one eye looking over his shoulder all the time, if you know what I mean.

I fill them in and Montana sounds sad when she says, "I wish we could go visit him at the hospital."

"Me, too," says Sam.

I wish we could, too. I mean, I hate aquariums because they catch whales and stuff and keep them in captivity and it makes them go crazy and die, but I also would have liked to see Jack Skye before he gets set free. The aquarium where they took him is on the mainland so we would have to take a ferry to get there. It just isn't practical, I can hear my mum saying in my head. She's not really saying it, I'm just thinking that that is what she would say, that's all.

"Maybe he'll come back to the island and see us

when they let him go!" I say hopefully.

Of course, just at that moment Mum starts yelling that dinner is ready, so I have to hang up.

Since Jenny has mostly left, I must say that dinner in this family has become a pretty sad thing. For example, tonight we are eating something called Tofu Something-or-Other. I'm sure you can imagine how delicious this is, if by delicious I mean horrendous. I eat a few bites and then try to hide the rest under my knife. The other kids are at their mum's, so naturally everyone is paying way too much attention to me, i.e. badgering me.

"How's math class going?" says Dad, cheerfully taking a giant bite of the stuff. Some sauce dribbles down from his mouth. Seriously gross. It's like watching Nicholas Zane baahing and barfing up milk. I nearly throw up just looking at him.

"Carly!" Mum says. "Stop fooling around and answer the question!" Like I'm doing something wrong. I take a sip of water to stop myself from being ill. I swish it a bit to get the tofu taste out of my mouth. Eating tofu reminds me a lot of eating glue, not that I've ever done this, but what I would imagine eating glue is like.

"Math is great," I say. Which isn't true. The fact is that I forgot to do my math homework on the weekend, at least partially because of being nearly dead from jellyfish stings, and I got in trouble and now I have a billion extra math questions to answer before the end of the week.

"I knew you'd start to like it once you began to understand it!" Dad says. "I loved math."

"I *know*," I say, and roll my eyes.

"Don't roll your eyes!" says Mum.

"Sorry," I tell her. Honestly, sometimes I can't do anything right. Right away, Mum starts telling a really exciting (not) story about how much the baby slept today and how brilliant he is, which is hilarious because all he does is eat and poo and sleep and cry. I mean, I guess he's pretty cute, but "brilliant" is pushing it. I don't interrupt her, though, because I don't much want to talk about math. I notice they don't ask me about diving, which is too bad, because I could tell them about how Jon is letting me and Sam try synchronized diving, which means we do the same dive at the same time and it looks really neat when we watch the playback. The problem is that I'm so tall that it takes me longer to do the twists and stuff and it's hard to get it right.

I manage to get away with dumping most of my meal on the floor, where Blue slurps it up. He's a garbage can, I swear. He'll eat anything. Never mind that I'm starving to death. I wonder if I could call Jenny and pay her my allowance to cook us dinner every night. She made such good dinners.

I sigh dramatically.

"What's the matter?" Mum asks.

"Nothing," I say. "My stings hurt. I'm going to lie down."

Which isn't exactly true, but if I tell them I have to do homework they'll bug me to *see* it and *help* with it, and that's just the worst. You know what I mean, right? Like it's bad enough that I have to *do* it, but to have them "help" makes me want to stick my pencil in my eye. And believe me, my face looks stupid enough without that.

I sit down on the floor of my room to do my homework. Something about sitting on the floor helps me, and besides, the computer takes up the whole desk. Also, it's a blistering hot day and it's cooler on the floor. I lie down and open my book, and before I can even answer one question, I accidentally fall asleep. I mean, I can't help it. It's been a long day.

I wake up with my face mushed into my math book, which I'm sure is just lovely. Maybe I absorbed a bunch of math while having bad dreams about jellyfish, but I doubt it. I sigh and stretch and look at the clock. Half an hour until bedtime. Oh no! I grab my notebook and try to do my homework as fast as I can. It might not all be right or anything, but at least I tried. Mr. Whatsit can't call me out for not trying. Hmmph. I actually work very hard at math. I'm just no good at it.

I'm concentrating so hard that I nearly have a heart attack when the phone rings. It's nearly bedtime! Who would phone this late?

"Hello?" I say.

"Is that Carly?" a voice says.

"No," I say, because there is only one person in the world with such an annoying voice. It's *Nigel*. Why is he phoning me? He might have woken me up. Also, he's the last person in the world I ever want to talk to.

"Um," he says, like he's nervous, which is hilarious.

"What do you want?" I say.

"I was just calling to see if you were all right," he says.

"You saw me yesterday," I say, giving away the fact that I'm me, but whatever. I did see him yesterday. He was in math class being obnoxiously smart and helpful, if by helpful I mean show-offy. He is a crazy freak of nature, really.

"I know," he says, "But I didn't have a chance to talk to you and . . . um . . . my dad said I should ring."

A-ha! A clue.

"Why?" I say, trying to sound like I'm not discovering a clue. "Because he feels responsible for my stings?"

"Why would he feel responsible for your stings?" says Nigel.

"I don't know," I say mysteriously. "I was just saying."

"That's a bit of a daft thing to say," he says.

"No, it isn't," I say.

"Actually, it is," he says.

"Look," I say, "I'm very busy right now. What do you want?"

"Oh," he says. "Um, I rang because I found out something about the jellyfish."

I casually say, "What?" as though I'm not writing down every word in case it turns that out my whole would-only-happen-in-a-movie idea turns out to be the actual truth.

"It's something to do with the weather," he says. "The water current is warmer this year and they came up in the current. They're all over the Gulf Islands. It was in the paper."

"A-ha!" I say. Which means, "Obviously you know all about them, seeing as you had something to do with them being there."

But *why* would they? And what would that have to do with shooting a seal and a porpoise? But never mind, I don't want to over-think it. I think there is something wrong with my brain vis-à-vis Nigel and his dad. Maybe I'm completely wrong about them. It's just that whenever I see Nigel (or hear his annoying voice) I get a suspicious feeling. I can't describe it, but it's bad. None of it makes sense.

"I have to go," I say and I hang up. Honestly, what did he phone for to begin with? I stuff my math books in my backpack and get my bathing suit ready for diving practice and crawl into bed. All night I have terrible nightmares about people shooting me because they think I'm a seal. Or a porpoise.

I blame Nigel. Really, he's annoying enough during the day, I wish he'd leave my nightmares alone.

I wake up on Thursday in your basic Terrible Mood. The sheets are all tangled around me because I was probably flailing around in a panic in my sleep. Also, I have to be at math in twenty minutes and I slept in. I stomp down to the kitchen and Mum and Dad are just sitting in there having a big old cup of coffee and chatting like nothing is up. Isn't it their job to wake me up for class? I mean, really. That's what parents are *for.*

"Did you see this?" Dad says, showing me an article in the newspaper about jellyfish.

"I don't have time!" I say, pushing it away, although I am very interested in reading it. "I'm *late.*"

"I'll drive you," says Mum. "What time are you supposed to be there?"

"What kind of mother are you that you don't

know?" I say, scratching my lip wildly. Honestly, between the leg/arm/belly itch from the jellyfish and the lip itch from the wasp, a girl could go crazy. "Argh!" I scream.

Which, of course, wakes up the baby.

"I'll get him," says Dad. "You just go to class."

"*Fine*," I say and stomp out to the car with some kind of crappy toaster pastry in my hand. I hate eating these things for breakfast. They're too sugary! You wouldn't catch an Olympic diver eating junk food, but I was desperate and also starving from not eating dinner last night.

Finally Mum gets into the car. I'm already late. Great.

"I'm glad we have a few minutes alone together," she says after we've driven for a bit. "I've been worrying about how you're coping with things."

"What things?" I say, chewing vigorously and getting crumbs all over her car floor.

"Oh," she says, "like the baby and stuff."

"It's *fine*," I say emphatically. I know all she thinks about is the baby. And what does she mean by "and stuff"? I have lots of other things on my mind other than him. Like, for example, *math*. And diving. And being taller than everyone else. And animals getting shot. And Nigel being a pain. And how my friends sometimes look at me like I'm too weird for them. And how they sometimes talk about me when I'm not around. I mean, obviously I don't know that they do this, but I'm pretty sure they do because sometimes they give each other these looks that say, "We've been talking about Carly behind her back!"

"Are you sure?" she says. "I know my attention has been a bit focused on him and I wanted to make sure that — "

"It's *fine*," I say again. "What do you want me to say? He's cute. He isn't making me upset."

"Good," she says. "Because you seem kind of cranky and I was just wondering if — "

"I have a *lot going on*," I yell. Luckily, we're at that moment pulling up in front of the ugly purple school. I jump out of the car and run inside before she can say anything more. If you are more than five minutes late, Mr. Whatsit makes you do an extra equation on the board at the front of the class. I'm mad at my mum for making me late, because of course he *does* give me an extra equation. And it's hard. It has fractions and negative numbers.

The class drags on and on and on for what can only be described as eternity, which means forever. I'm sure I've aged like at least twelve years in this horrible bad-smelling classroom. Now that I've been to a few classes, I'm starting to notice that although none of the kids seems to know (or like) each other, they all have one thing in common: they are as dumb as dirt. I feel as hostile towards them as I'm sure they do towards me.

"Carly," Mr. Whatsit says after The Most Horrible Math Class ever, breathing his bad breath all over my head, "Nigel is going to give you an extra tutoring session to help you with your homework because I think you're getting a bit behind."

I roll my eyes, although inside my head I think I must be screaming. "Fine," I say. "Great. Thanks so much. I'm sure that will be just swell. But now I'm late. I have to go to Diving Camp."

I want him to know that I'm not just all about math. I have a life! I have other things going on!

Nigel looks over at me and winks. *Winks.* The horror!

"Argh!" I scream so loudly that Mr. Whatsit drops his book on his foot, which probably hurts. He winces, anyway.

"What time should I ring you, Carly?" says Nigel.

"Look," I say. "I'm sure this is all very ducky, but I'm late for Diving Camp and I have to go, so I'll see you tomorrow." I smile as sweetly as I can, but with my eyes I try to communicate to them both exactly how I feel about math, which backfires horribly because Nigel yells, "I'll ring you later!"

Oh, goody.

If by goody I mean ugh.

"Hi, Carly," says Sam. I'm so relieved to see her I nearly hug her, even though she probably wouldn't want to hug me because my skin looks so awful and gross.

"Hi," I say. Sometimes I swear the only people I like in the whole world are Sam, Felicia, Montana and of course, Jon, but that's because he looks like a movie star and he's a really good diver.

"Did you see the story about the jellyfish in the paper?" she says. "My mum cut it out for you."

"That's nice," I say through gritted teeth. Obviously, the Jellyfish Mystery has already been solved. Great.

"So it wasn't Nigel," she points out. "And whatever you were saying about him bringing jellyfish from England made you sound like a crazy person."

"I'm not crazy!" I say.

"I know," she says. "I'm just saying."

"What?"

"What what?"

"What are you just saying?"

"What?" she says. "What are you talking about?"

"Okay," I say. "I give up." I feel very tired and a slight bit mean towards her. What is she talking about? I know I sounded crazy! It's Nigel's fault. Nigel is making me crazy. The fact that I'm even thinking about him again is making me want to stick my head in the water for a good long time.

Jon comes over to where we are standing on the pool deck. "Are you girls going to dive today or are you just going to chat?" he says, in the way he says stuff which loosely means, "Get to work!"

"We're diving!" we both yelp at once and jump right into the pool and start our warm-ups. We warm up by doing a set of stretches and stuff and then we swim some laps. I love swimming laps because it always puts me in less of a bad mood and clears my head. The swimming pool is so pretty in the summer and sun shines in through all the glass and makes the water look super turquoise-blue, which is my new favourite colour in the world. Also, while you're swimming laps, you have lots of time to think about stuff.

It's obvious, I think, that I'm wrong about Nigel and his dad putting the jellyfish in the bay on purpose. And that even saying that out loud made me seem like a nutter butter. I'm sad that we won't be swimming at the cabin this year, though. I mean, who wants to take that chance? And what will we do if we can't swim? We'll have to go for walks in the woods instead and everyone knows that the woods aren't nearly as interesting as the sea. Maybe we can get Dad to teach us how to sail in the little sabot he built, which is like a dinghy but with a sail. Then we could be in the water! But not swimming. Or diving.

Really, the cabin is proving very dangerous, although it's still my favourite place in the world.

I swim a few extra laps because it's so pretty and I can't seem to stop. By the time I'm done, I'm in a much better mood and Sam is already up on the platform. She waves at me right before she does her dive, which is totally perfect. She's such a good diver. I wish I could say I was a better diver than her, but I don't think I am anymore. Which kind of bums me out, but what can you do? She's one of my best friends so I have to be happy for her. I slowly climb up the ladder to the top for my turn. Jon has given me instructions on what I'm supposed to be doing, which is a dive from a handstand, which I'm very good at by the way, and that's pretty much what I'm thinking about. And it's kind of bugging me a small bit that I won't be as good as Sam is at the same thing.

I like to be the best of everyone, which I know is show-offy. Don't think I don't know! I'm working on it, okay?

By the time I get to the top of the ladder, I'm totally winded from all the lap swimming and the climbing. I'm in really good shape, but I still get tired. I'm a little out of breath when I get to the end and get ready. I'm going to do a twist right off the top, which is hard, but not that hard. I mean, I've done it a kajillion times. So I go into a hand-stand and I concentrate really super hard on getting it perfect. We had a sports guy come and speak to us one day and he talked about how you have to picture it perfectly in your head and don't think about what might go wrong because if you picture what might go wrong, then it will go wrong because you'll do the last thing you pictured in your head. Just thinking about him makes me picture myself falling off the board altogether and missing the water so I try to erase that by doing my shake-my-head trick.

I'm just about ready to go, my fingers curling over the edge of the concrete, when I hear it.

Buzzing.

I look around as much as I can without falling over and I see a wasp coming right towards me! I can't get stung again! My lip is only just starting to look normal to me! I snap my hand at it and of course I lose my balance, and I don't think I've ever been so scared except maybe that time that Montana hurt her back at the cabin diving off the rock and I'm kind of falling into the water.

I hit the water with a bang, which doesn't actually hurt as much as I thought it would. I mean, falling off the tower is a long way. When you are standing up there, it looks like a million kabillion miles to the water. I've always been scared of falling. Earlier this year, I started to get dizzy and panicky up there on the platform and I thought I was going to have to stop.

But now I've fallen, and it wasn't so bad. Funny, huh.

I start to swim for the edge, expecting Jon to yell at me for belly-flopping, even though I didn't, when I notice that the water is going all red around me.

I'm bleeding! I'm bleeding!

And Jon is there pulling me out and saying, "I think it looks worse than it is!"

And I realize I must have bumped my head on the edge of the platform on the way down, which makes me a bit proud because I saw that in the Olympics once, so in a way it's kind of cool that I did it and it didn't really hurt.

Or at least, that's what I thought until I get into the first-aid room and look in the mirror.

There's a huge cut on my forehead! Sam pokes her head in. "Oh my gosh, are you okay?" she says.

"Yes!" I say, trying to be brave. But really, it looks like someone cut my head open with a can opener. It goes all across my forehead! Cassie comes running in because she's the first-aid person and right away she says, "I'm going to take you to the hospital."

I swear, I've had enough of hospitals to last me a lifetime, but I follow her to her car. My head doesn't really hurt at all, which is the most peculiar thing.

"I don't think you have a concussion," she says. "Do you have ringing in your ears?"

"No!" I say. "I feel fine."

"Good," she says. "It's just that there's lots of blood around your scalp, so it bleeds a lot."

I can tell she's trying not to look worried. We get to the hospital and I get let in right away, which apparently is really lucky because there are about a hundred people sitting in the waiting room coughing and looking forlorn. Poor sick people! I hope they don't give me germs.

A doctor comes in right away and examines me by asking me difficult questions. Some of them are math.

"I hate math!" I say. "I wish people would stop asking me math questions."

"I think she's okay," says Cassie.

Meanwhile, they've cleaned up my head and the doctor goes ahead and stitches it up. Now, I have to say the whole "stitching it up" process was the grossest thing that I've ever been a part of. I mean, think about it. He's sewing up my HEAD! Afterwards, he puts a big bandage over it, but not before I see a big row of black stitches. I look like Frankenstein! A monster! I almost cry, but not quite. After all, it didn't really hurt. Not that much, anyway. Well, maybe a bit.

"Oh my *God*," says Mum when Cassie takes me home. "What *happened?*"

She looks close to crying herself, as well she should. I mean, so far, since the baby came home, I've been stung by a bee, a wasp and some jellyfish. And now I have Frankenstein's forehead. I glare at her, which makes me feel guilty because she looks really upset.

"It doesn't hurt!" I tell her.

"There's no concussion," Cassie tells her. "She just cut her head on the edge of the platform. The doctor said it looks worse than it is."

"Oh, thank goodness," says Mum, hugging me so hard I nearly fall over. "My poor baby."

"She'll be okay," says Cassie.

"I will, Mum," I say, struggling out of her arms. "It's just a surface wound."

"You poor thing," says Mum. Which, actually, I don't mind that much. And I mind even less when she lets me skip my math homework and I get to choose a movie and pizza instead. Which is the best. My favourite thing in the world. Well, except for the cabin.

And diving, of course.

I don't even mind so much that Nicholas Zane cries for half the movie and that Mum falls asleep in the middle and starts snoring. I feel a bit sorry for her, kind of. I mean, she shouldn't think it's her fault that I'm accident-prone. So I make her a nice card to find when she wakes up. It has a drawing on it of her holding NZ and sleeping and inside it says, *Thanks for being such a great mum.*

I hope she likes it. I hope she knows it means that I'm not totally mad at her all the time, it just sort of seems that way lately. I hope she gets what I mean.

chapter 8

"Hi, nice to meet you, I'm Frankenstein," I say, crossing my eyes.

Montana laughs. "Carly, that's not funny," she says.

Why do people always say something's not funny after they laugh? That doesn't make any sense. I make a scary face and say, "Yes, it is."

It's a gorgeous Saturday afternoon (it took forever to get going this morning because of little NZ) and I'm sitting at the end of the dock at the marina, dangling my feet into the water.

"Look," she says. "Fish!" She peers over the edge so far I think she's going to fall in, so I grab the back of her sweater and pull her back. I'm very nervous about accidents. I should change my name to Accident Girl. Also, my stitches are itchy. I don't know if you know this, but there is nothing worse than itchy stitches. If you scratch them, for example, they might come off or pull out and then your wound might open back up again. I'd say more about it but just thinking about it makes my stomach do a somersault.

Speaking of somersaults makes me think of gymnastics. Finally, the other day, my mum asked me about gymnastics. Like she *just* noticed that I stopped going? That's crazy, it's been weeks. I thought she'd be mad but she just said, "I think your diving is more important to you, Carly, and I'm proud of you for making a choice." I mean, whatever. It strikes me as a funny thing to say.

I stand up and do a backwards walkover on the dock.

"Carly!" squeals Montana. It makes me a little sad because she used to do backwards walkovers with me but then she got hurt and now she can't. She wouldn't have got hurt if it weren't for me. I think I'm a "getting hurt" magnet. You know how some people are good-luck magnets? My dad says that our neighbour across the street is a good-luck magnet because he got all the lottery numbers right. He still works, though. He's a golf pro and he loves it so he says he'll work forever. Only now he drives a nicer car. I don't know why he doesn't move to a bigger, nicer house. If I won a million dollars, I'd get a house with a proper-sized swimming pool in the back and a bunch of diving boards of different heights, proper ones, so I could practise.

I lie down on the dock and Montana lies next to me and we can smell the ocean water and Roo's terrible breath and also the cedar of the dock and the creosote smell of that black stuff they put on wood so it doesn't rot.

"That one looks like a man's head!" she says, pointing at a white puffy cloud.

"It looks like Mr. Whatsit," I tell her. "Only without the giant *wart* on his nose."

She giggles. "Does he really have a wart?"

"No," I admit. "But he has the kind of personality where he should have a wart on his nose. People like him should be warty. The math people."

"Hey!" says Montana as Blue licks her face. "Gross."

"It's not gross," I say. "It's a kiss. He's kissing you."

"Ew," she says, and we kind of fall about laughing. I can't explain it, but sometimes you just get the giggles so hard that you have to roll around, even though you're already lying down. Which after a few minutes hurts my stomach muscles more than Cassie's sit-up drill, I can tell you. I kind of am gasping for breath like a laughing fish or something when I hear Sam and Felicia's footsteps running down the dock. Mum and Dad are right behind them with what's left of the load of stuff for the weekend. Marly and Shane aren't with us this weekend and the baby has been sleeping this whole time in his stroller just beside us. We were supposed to watch him, but there isn't much to see when he's lying there asleep. He's basically just like a sausage. Well, a sausage with eyes, a nose and a mouth and some hair that's starting to get a bit cute and curly.

I wish I had curly hair. My hair is straight and when I got my stitches, Mum insisted on cutting my bangs so they didn't tickle the stitches and now I have the world's shortest bangs. Seriously, these bangs wouldn't look good on anyone. I look around jealously at my friends' perfect hair: Felicia has long dark curls and Sam has nice blond hair and Montana has stick-straight black shiny hair that you can practically see yourself in, it's that shiny. It's crazy how shiny it is. "Are you coming, Carly?" Dad says and I see that everyone else is on the boat already. Oops. I was all caught up inside my own head. That happens sometimes.

Finally we're off! The girls and I sit below with the baby and Mum sits up top with Dad. This gives us time to come up with a plan. The New Plan. For how we are going to catch Nigel and his dad doing Bad Things, such as shooting seals and porpoises. We are all wearing sort of matching pale pink sweatshirts. What happened was that the girls liked mine so much they all went out and got their own pink sweatshirts, although Montana's is sort of more purple than pink, and I gave them iron-on pictures of Jack Skye to put on the back. They look very cool, I must say, even though I designed the picture on them so I shouldn't feel like they are as cool as I think they are because that's sort of like bragging.

"I wonder if we'll get into the paper when we solve the crime!" Sam says, nudging Felicia. "Like the gang in the Scooby-Doo movies."

"For sure," giggles Felicia. "We'll be famous!" Maybe I'm wrong, but I think she rolls her eyes a bit. Felicia is NOT a sarcastic person. I shoot her a look, but she doesn't look back at me. Huh.

"We have to solve it first," says Montana.

"Well," I say, "first of all, we need to find some more clues." I scratch my arm, which is still itchy from the jellyfish stings. "And we'll have lots of time," I add, "because you won't want to go swimming with all those jellyfish in the water."

"Maybe Nigel and his dad won't be there," says Sam. "Then we can look around their cabin. For, like, guns and stuff." Wait, is she being sarcastic too? Suddenly it seems like maybe my friends are making fun of me. But I'm sure they aren't. I mean, what kind of friends would do that?

"What if they *are* there?" says Felicia.

"Then we'll spy on them," I say.

Montana writes it all down in her book. Spy and Cabin. It looks very professional.

"We could ask them questions and see if they

get all flustered," she says. "If they do, then they're probably lying."

"Good idea," I say. "But then we'd have to talk to Nigel. Ew!" I make a face and giggle. No one else laughs. I don't know why. I squint at them suspiciously. Maybe they are in cahoots with Nigel and his father. No, that's crazy. Maybe they are just weirdos.

"Just how well do any of you know Nigel, anyway?" I say.

Sam shrugs. "Not at all. He goes to your school, not mine."

"Don't know him," says Felicia. "I've seen him. He's sort of cute."

Sam giggles. "Is he cute?" she asks Montana.

"Sort of," says Montana, without looking me in the eye. What a traitor! She's gone over to his side! She has a crush on him!

"He's not cute," I say definitively. I mean, really. These girls are crazy.

We spend the rest of the boat trip making pictures of maps with trails showing the fastest route from our cabin to Nigel's cabin and also the trickiest route and the route with the most hiding places. Really, we're very thorough. It's good to have a plan.

"It's good to have a plan," says Montana, which is weird because it was exactly what I was just thinking, in the exact words even. It's so creepy when things like that happen. I think it means something magical, like we're on the same wavelength or something, so I try thinking something really loudly in my own head, which is specifically, "Nigel has cooties," and Montana says, "I think Nigel's accent is nice."

Huh.

So we aren't on the same wavelength at all. I frown at her, which makes my stitches feel itchy and pully. I tap on the bandage with my finger. Being sewn up is so funny. You can feel all your skin tugging when you move your face.

"I see the island!" yells Sam.

We all look out the window, and there it is. My heart is lub-lubbing because no matter how many times we come here, it's always as exciting as ever. And besides, this time we've got a job to do.

We get all the stuff hauled up the hill in record time, which earns us a root beer and some cookies. I love root beer the best of all. It just tastes the best. And cold root beer on a hot day is better than best. I teach them all how to blow into their pop cans so the pop doesn't spill out and so they don't get stung on the lip by a bee or a wasp. I can attest to the fact that it hurts.

We blow into our cans and make pop-can music until Mum says, "Why don't you girls go for a walk and burn off all that energy instead of just sitting around being noisy?"

Which makes us laugh, because it was funny the way she said it, and Montana goes, "Let's take the map!" So we know that our adventure is truly beginning.

"Let's take the fastest path," says Sam, leading the way. "Then we'll know right away if they're there or not."

"If we don't take a path at all," says Felicia, "then we can walk along the beach and look up at their cabin and know if they're there, and if they are, we can keep walking like we're just going for a walk and not like we're spying on them."

"The path is quicker," says Montana.

I'm kind of torn. Because I agree with Felicia, but Montana is my best friend.

"What do you think, Carly?" says Montana.

"Um," I say. "I guess the fast path." I look at Felicia as if to say, "I'm sorry, I thought your idea was better but I have to take my best friend's side," and she gives me a funny look back which either says, "What are you talking about?" or "There's something hanging out of your nose." Honestly, I wish all this thought-talking was easier.

We set off through the woods, which is all quiet and has long shadows because it's very late in the afternoon, probably almost dinnertime. I love the smell of the woods even though I don't really care for going for long walks. Luckily, this one isn't very far via the fast path. We whisper our plans back and forth in case someone overhears us. It's too bad that we couldn't just think them really loudly and read what each other was thinking, but if that was possible, what would stop other people who aren't supposed to be reading your thoughts from reading your thoughts? It probably wouldn't work.

"Argh!" screams Sam suddenly from up ahead. That gets my attention.

"What?" I say. "What?"

"Cobweb," she says, making spitting sounds. I guess she got face-webbed, which is the worst. I mean it. I'm not scared of spiders — well, okay, I'm terrified of them. And walking face first into a cobweb and getting all that sticky thread stuck in your hair makes you feel like a billion spiders are crawling all over you. I go help her wipe it off.

"Use a spider stick," I tell her.

"What's a spider stick?" she says.

So I show her. A spider stick is what I call a stick that you carry in front of your face to stop any spider stuff from getting on you when you're the first one walking along a path.

"Neat," she says, waving it in front of her face.

"Yeah," giggles Montana. "And it's also good for scaring bears away."

"Bears?" says Felicia, looking afraid.

"There are no bears here," I assure her. "Believe

me, there are no bears or cougars or wolves on this whole island. Only a few sheep and some deer."

The part about the sheep is funny because you wouldn't expect sheep to be on an island like this, but the fact is that someone brought sheep here about a million years ago, probably when Brother XII had all his followers here and in between burying pots of gold (not), they raised sheep and stuff and when they left, they left the sheep behind and now they are wild sheep. Only they aren't wild sheep in the way that you would picture proper wild sheep. They are just regular sheep with really matted fur and a demented look in their eyes, probably from eating nothing but salal bushes and stinging nettle for their whole lives. Anyway, once in a while you'll be walking down a path and you'll hear a thundering sound like a train coming and a mottled herd of these wild-but-not-wild sheep will come stampeding out of nowhere and practically knock you over and trample you to death with their hard feet.

"Shh!" says Sam dramatically, waving her hands around a bit, which makes her look like she's overacting in a play. I give her a funny look and then I see that we are almost right behind Nigel's cabin. It looks pretty quiet, but really, how can you tell if someone is home or not? There is no electricity or TV or anything on this island, so people's places tend to be quiet whether they are there or not, except ours of course, which is crazy noisy with the baby crying and the little kids yelling.

We tiptoe as close as we dare, and Felicia pokes her nose up and peers in a window. "It's empty!" she calls.

"Good," says Sam, taking out her camera.

"What are you doing?" I ask her.

"Taking pictures," she says, joining Felicia at the window and aiming her camera inside. She snaps a whole bunch of pictures. "We can blow them up on the computer later."

I giggle. "We don't have a computer here," I point out. "There's no electricity!"

"We could just look right now with our own eyes," says Montana, writing something down. I wish I knew what she was writing down. Honestly, I think she's been acting a bit funny ever since she admitted she thinks Nigel is cute. She's probably writing her name with his inside a heart or something stupid like that. Or did she find a clue that she isn't telling the rest of us about? That's the problem with having a gang — you never know when one person in your gang is going to take over the whole thing. Or start rooting for the Bad Guys.

"What did you write down?" I ask.

"Nothing," she says.

"Huh," I say. I mean, I saw her write something, so obviously she's hiding something from me. *And* she thinks Nigel has a cute accent, which makes her a Person of Suspicion in my book. If I'd brought my own notebook, I'd have written it down myself, but I didn't bring it. I forgot it at home, to tell you the honest to Pete truth. I peer through the window and lo and behold, there is a book about porpoises on the table! Very suspicious! As if that wasn't enough evidence, there is a notebook open on the floor and there is a drawing of a porpoise on the page. A-HA!

"Over here!" yells Sam. "They've got all kinds of dolphin stuff in there! Maybe Carly's actually right!" She's gone up onto the deck, which is a brave thing to do because it's almost like trespassing, although trespassing rules are different for cabins than for houses. After all, last winter when we were caught here in a storm, we even broke into a cabin (not this one) with my dad and ate all their canned food and slept in their sleeping bags. Which was okay and fine and whatever with the owners because Dad called them when we got back into town and explained. They were really nice and said they were glad we got shelter in their cabin. But think about it — I mean, if you were in the city one day and you were out and about and there was a snowstorm, I don't think very many people would be happy that you broke into their house and ate their assortment of soup and spaghetti. That would be wrong. Probably you'd go to jail.

I go up on the deck with the others for a better view of the clues. Also, what does "Maybe Carly's actually right?" mean? That they've just been pretending to believe me all this time? Huh. I can feel a bubble of madness starting but I try to ignore it. There isn't even a light for me to stare at or whatnot so I just swallow it down. Now is not the time for me to get mad. After all, we are trespassing for clues, which is more important than the fact that my friends don't believe anything I say.

If we get caught, I guess we could say that we were just looking for Nigel to come out and play with us, which is hilarious and makes me laugh out loud because Nigel is the last person I would ever invite to come out and play with me, but you know what I mean.

The deck of their cabin is old and falling apart. Obviously they bought this place from someone who never came here and looked after it. Dad is always building new decks at our cabin, so ours is safe to walk on, for example, without plunging your foot through . . . which is exactly what happens.

"Help!" I scream as my leg goes through the wood. It hurts like mad, I don't mind telling you.

"What happened?" says Felicia, running over to me.

"I'm stuck!" I say. Which is true, I realize, as I try to pull my foot out of the hole. I actually don't think I'm wounded, I'm just stuck almost all the way up to my hip.

"Do you want us to pull you?" says Montana.

Sam takes a picture. "What are you DOING?" I yell.

"I took a picture," she says.

"I know *that*," I say. "I just thought it was mean."

"Don't get mad," she says. "Do you want help or not?"

"I want help," I say. They all grab a part of my arms and stuff and start pulling, which hurts more than if they didn't.

"STOP!" I yell, which they do. I feel very mad at them, even though it's not their fault that I fell through the deck.

"You almost pulled my arms clean out of their sockets," I say. "Be careful."

"You're heavy," says Felicia.

"No, I'm not," I tell her. "I'm a very normal weight for my height."

"Well, you're tall," says Sam.

"I *know*," I say.

I can feel tears plonging against the backs of my eyes, not because it hurts but because I feel stupid *and* mad. How can I not go an entire day without hurting myself? And now I'm stuck on Nigel's deck forever. And probably my friends don't even care.

"Oh no," says Montana, just at that moment. "Look!" She points down the beach, and, of course, guess who's coming towards us?

Obviously.

Nigel and his dad.

"Run!" says Felicia, and they all take off running in the direction of the woods. Whoa, wait a minute! What kind of friends are they? How could they all run off and leave me? I mean, I know they're freaking out and whatnot because we are going to get caught, but how could they actually *leave* me here? It's the worst thing imaginable. I'm deserted! I'm abandoned! Who would do that to a person?

I can see Montana sort of hesitating and making to come back so I decide to be all heroic and I take a deep breath and then I gesture to her to go. She might as well desert me, too. Why not?

I decide right then that I am going to take the fall for my friends, because I'm nice and that is what a nice person would do, and besides, it might make them like me better again instead of sort of rolling their eyes all the time when they think I'm not looking. Montana makes a face as if to say, "Are you sure? I can't abandon you!" And I make a face that says, "Yes, go." Then I shout, "Go! Go!" so she's clear.

Actually, I sort of wanted her to stay, but then

I did tell her to go, even if I really actually didn't mean it.

When she's gone, I push at the deck desperately and pull at my leg, but I'm totally stuck. What are Nigel and his dad going to think? I'm beside myself, as I'm sure you can imagine.

"Carly?" says Nigel, coming up onto the deck. He's a bit out of breath, like he's been running. Hmmm, I think to myself. Probably running after some seal or otter on the beach to shoot. Or a porpoise. I squint at him carefully to see if he's carrying a gun. "Carly?" he says again.

"That's my name," I shoot back. "Don't wear it out." Which I think is quite witty if I do say so myself. Of course, I haven't actually explained how I came to be hip-deep in his deck. I shoot him a defiant look.

"Your head still looks awful," he says.

"Gee, thanks," I tell him. I think it's a little weird that his first comment wouldn't be, "Gee, Carly, I can't help but wonder why you're stuck in my deck up to your hip!" Maybe this happens all the time. Maybe it's some sort of elaborate trap that he and his dad have worked out to prevent people from spying on their Porpoise-Shooting Operation. Or maybe he just likes telling me that I look awful. Huh.

"Are you going to help me out or not?" I say finally.

I mean, I want help, but I don't want him yanking on my arms. His dad appears behind him. "Oh, hi, Carly," he says. "How are those stings healing up?" Which makes me blush furiously because I've just remembered that I found out that the stuff that they threw on my stings was *pee!* I didn't ask whose pee it was. Apparently, if you throw pee on a jellyfish sting, it can take the sting away and it's all they had to use as a neutralizer. Maybe it was Nigel's dad's pee! Isn't that the grossest thing ever?

"Gross," I say.

"Your stings are gross?" he says. "Did they get infected?"

"I didn't say 'gross,'" I say, which I know is weird because I did say it, but to tell you the truth, this entire day is so weird I may as well be weird to go along with it.

Nigel's dad reaches over. "I see you fell into our trap!" he says, laughing, and he plucks me up like I weigh nothing and plonks me down on the ground with both feet down. My leg wobbles for a minute and I nearly fall over, but I don't.

A-HA! I think. He admits it was a trap.

"You admit it was a trap!" I yell.

"Um," says Nigel, "I think he was kidding. Our humour is so much different than yours."

"Right," I say, rolling my eyes. Nigel once told me that I wouldn't understand his jokes because

British humour is sophisticated and North American humour isn't. "Ha ha," I add. "You crazy British people are a laugh a minute."

Eventually, after like a second, I feel dumb standing there. They're both kind of looking at me expectantly.

Finally his dad says, "Well, I'm going in to start making dinner."

"What are you making?" I ask quickly, sensing an opportunity for clue gathering. "Did you hunt some seals today?"

"Ha ha ha," he laughs merrily, like I've said the funniest thing in the world. That wasn't the reaction that I was looking for, but I guess it illustrates how distinctly unfunny British people can be.

"Ha ha," I say, to be agreeable. "Well, I have to go. It's been a slice," I add.

"Nigel will walk you home," he says, disappearing inside.

Nigel grins at me.

"I don't need you to walk me home," I hiss. "I'm totally capable of walking on my own."

To demonstrate, I stride off towards the woods, which is not actually as easy as I thought because I must have twisted my ankle when I fell through the floor. I take about a step and a half and then I fall over.

"I can see that," he says. "Maybe I'll just come along and make sure you don't hurt yourself too much. We can talk about maths. I mean, math. After all, I am your tutor."

"Shut up," I say. "I never want your help again in a million billion years."

"You're very hostile," he says. "It's a bit bizarre."

"You're very rude," I say.

"I'm only coming with you to save you from danger," he says.

"Like you'd be able to save me anyway," I say. Honestly, I'm so mad at my friends for abandoning me here that I could just scream or spit or both. I still can't believe they just *left*. They're probably back at the cabin having ice cream floats and admiring each others' hair. For all they know, I've been kidnapped, or worse. I didn't *mean* they should go! I meant that I should tell them to go and then they should stay anyway. It's hard to explain, but I would have thought they would have understood. I decide right then and there never to invite them to the cabin again. I look into the woods. It is getting a bit dark. Maybe I'll let Nigel come along just in case there's a stampede of wild sheep. Then I can save myself by pushing him in front of them.

"Fine," I say. "Just don't talk to me."

We walk a little bit. Or he walks and I sort of hop.

"Do you like shooting animals in the sea?" I say, to make conversation.

"You told me not to talk to you," he says. "And what a silly question. Did you hit your head again when you fell through our deck?"

"No," I say. "I was just wondering about your hobbies."

"Do you know many people who have a hobby of shooting animals in the sea?" he says, frowning at me.

"No," I say. "Not really." I start humming to indicate that the conversation is over, and just at the part where I am humming the chorus, which is the best bit, I hear a loud bang. I don't mind telling you that it makes me fall over. Is Nigel shooting me?

"Did you just shoot me?" I yell.

"No!" he says, staring at me. "What is *wrong* with you? That gunshot came from far away. But I wonder what it was? Gosh! I wish we could see from here." He runs over to a tree and starts climbing it, which is pretty funny because the tree is so skinny it just bends over so that he's nearly on the ground again when he gets to the top. He jumps off and it sproings back up again. I giggle.

"Did you see anything?" I say.

"No," he admits. "I think the sound came from the sea, though!"

"The Porpoise Shooter!" I blurt, without thinking. I mean, I don't want to tell Nigel about the case because then maybe he'll know I'm on to him. On the other hand, it couldn't have been him because he's here with me in the woods. It's hard for me to accept, but maybe — just maybe — Nigel is not actually a sea-animal murderer. Well, he can't be. I guess that's that then. Huh.

I look around. I don't even know what trail we are on, to tell you the truth. I wasn't paying attention. "What trail is this?" I say.

"I don't know," he says. "I was following you. Who on earth is the Porpoise Shooter?"

"I don't know what you mean," I say.

"Carly," he says. "Stop being strange."

"I'm not being strange," I say, mimicking his accent. It's hard not to, to tell you the truth. I don't know what's wrong with me. Am I turning British? "Are we lost?"

"We aren't lost," he says. "We're on a trail."

"But where does it go?" I say.

"To your cabin?" he says.

"I don't think so," I say.

"Come on," he says. "We won't get to the end unless we keep walking." Which frankly does not sound like the kind of advice you'd get in a How To Survive in the Woods book, but I follow him anyway. We walk for another twenty minutes or so with him badgering me the whole time about the Porpoise Shooter. Honestly, he's driving me crazy. He drives me crazier than Marly and Shane combined. He drives me the craziest of crazy.

"Fine!" I finally yell, slumping over on a mossy rock. Mossy rocks are the most comfortable for sitting on — you just have to make sure they are mossy rocks and not anthills. Believe me, I've made *that* mistake and I won't do it again. So I tell him about the seal who was shot, and Jack Skye.

"Wait," he says. "Who is Jack Skye?"

"The porpoise," I say. "Duh." Then I realize that of course he doesn't know who Jack Skye is, so I feel a bit bad about the "duh," but it's not as though I can take it back. So I just say again, "Jack Skye is a porpoise." I can tell he's really shocked because he goes pale.

"My dad's a porpoise researcher," he says. "He'll be really upset when he finds out one was shot."

"A porpoise researcher," I repeat.

"Yes," he says. "That's why we're here."

"Well," I say. "We were all upset about Jack Skye."

"I bet," he says. For a second, I forget that I hate him.

"We should go," he says, "I think it's going to get dark soon."

Which is all very well for him to say. My ankle is the size of a balloon, if the balloon was the size of a cantaloupe. "I don't know how much further I can walk," I say. "Why didn't we take the quick path?"

"I didn't know there was a quick path," he says. "You didn't tell me."

"Whatever," I say irritably. I'm starting to remember why I don't like him.

I get up like I know where I'm going and try to remember which way the sunset is from the cabin. Then I kind of point myself in that direction.

"I think we should go off the trail," I say, "And just walk this way."

"Okay," he says. Honestly, he'll agree with anything. But whatever. There isn't much undergrowth so it's pretty easy to walk through the woods — or, it would be if my ankle didn't kill me with every step. He takes the lead. "You're a slowpoke," he says. "I should have let you come home by yourself."

Which was really uncalled for as far as I'm concerned. Why is he getting grouchy? Getting grouchy is *my* job when we're lost in the woods. But I let him go first so he can break all the cobwebs with his dumb face. I don't even tell him about spider sticks, I just let him go. I'm just about to say something about his grouchiness when he stops so quickly that I walk-hop right into his back and we both nearly fall over.

"Wha—?" I start to say, and then I see what he's looking at.

I blink really hard because I think I must be imagining it, and then my heart starts going so fast that it must be about to shoot out of my chest and into my stomach and possibly into my feet or right out of my eye or something. It's crazy. Because standing right in front of us, looking right at us, is a really big cat.

To be exact, it's a cougar.

"There are no cougars here," I whisper.

"Shut up!" he says. "We don't want it to notice us."

But it does notice us. It's looking right at us, for one thing. How could it miss us? We aren't exactly small and camouflaged.

"I think we're supposed to scare it off," I whisper.

"How?" he whispers. He's really pale and I can't help but notice that he's shaking. I think he's more scared than me, which makes me feel braver even though I'm about to drop dead from fright.

"Like this," I tell him, reaching down for a big stick and swinging it around my head.

"ARGH!" I scream really loud.

"What are you doing?" he says.

I wave the stick around. "Make yourself big," I say. "Make yourself noisy!"

I start singing at the top of my lungs. It's a very annoying song that I hear all the time on the radio and I don't even like, but it doesn't matter. I hear him start singing along and I can see his stick swinging with mine.

The cougar just looks at us like we're very odd. I wish I could know what he was thinking because it would be nice to know if it was "Gosh, I wish my dinner would stop singing so I could eat it," or, "I'm frightened of these large singing beasts; I think I'll run away."

"Start walking backwards," I tell Nigel.

"Okay," he says.

We step backwards through the woods, which is harder than you might think because we keep walking backwards into trees and stuff. We're singing like crazy. We sing the national anthem and that super-annoying song from *Annie*. We sing everything in the world, it feels like. Finally the cougar disappears from view. I don't know if he's still standing there or if he ran off or if he just went around us so he could leap on us, but I'm too scared to think about it much. We burst through the woods at the beach, which happens to be the very bottom of the hill where my cabin is. I don't know where we were in the woods, but frankly, at this point I don't care. How could I get lost on my own island? That's too embarrassing to even admit. I think we walked in straight and then out straight and it took ages instead of a normal length of time.

Somehow, being able to see the cabin makes me feel safer.

"Blue!" I scream. "Roo!" And they come tumbling down the hill towards us and we start running up towards them and safety. My legs are shaking like crazy and I can't even feel my sore ankle. That's how scared I am. It's like my ankle was instantly healed the second I got scared. We run all the way up the hill, which is no small feat, and burst into the cabin.

"Finally!" says Mum. "We were starting to worry! The girls said you would be back soon, and you've been ages. Your dad was just about to come looking!"

"Cougar!" I gasp. "Cougar!" Which makes everyone gather around talking at once. "What cougar? What do you mean?" "I wish I'd been there with my camera, lucky bums." (Which was Sam, obviously.) And, "I'm never letting you walk in the woods alone again!" (My mum.) And, "I thought there were no cougars here." (My dad.)

So we tell the whole story from the beginning and then Dad takes Nigel home in the dinghy so he doesn't have to walk through the woods. Dad's gone a lot longer than we thought he'd be, and when he gets back, the night gets even stranger, because he comes in the door and says, "You won't believe it, but Nigel's dad caught some kids out in an aluminum runabout shooting at animals on the reef!"

"The Porpoise Shooter!" we all say at once.

I'm too relieved at not being Cougar Dinner to

be mad that my suspicions were all wrong. Because now it's really sinking in: Our Chief Suspect *caught* the Bad Guys. But then I do get a little bit mad. Okay, a lot mad. It's possible that I burst into tears.

"I know, Carly," my mum says, hugging me. "It's been a lot for one day."

"Yeah," I say. "It's been a lot."

Which is like the understatement of the century, if you don't mind me saying so.

"I'm glad the cougar didn't eat you," says Montana as we're just getting ready for bed.

"Me, too," I say. Then, "Why didn't you guys wait for me?" I don't want to tell her how mad I was that she left, even though I told her to, because I'm afraid that I'm going to start crying.

"I thought you told me *not* to!" she says, looking upset. "Oh, Carly. Oh . . . I feel really bad. I wanted to stay! I thought you wanted me to go." And then she starts crying and so do Sam and Felicia, and then we're all crying.

"I'm sorry," they all say.

And I say, "It's not your fault there was a cougar in the woods," which is true, and we all fall asleep.

chapter 9

July is shooting by so fast I can't stand it. It's whizzing. It's only half over, really, but still it seems like it's almost the end.

Anyway, the girls all got together and got me a present. It was totally out of the blue. I couldn't have been any more surprised. Well, I guess I could, but it was still nice. I think they feel bad about how they left me stuck in Nigel's deck and made me walk home by myself that day in the woods — or at least with just Nigel the Useless for companionship — so they got together and bought me a big poster that has a cougar on it for my half-birthday. Like it's almost six months from my actual birthday. I've never heard of a half-birthday but it's a really nice poster in any event.

Okay, the truth is that looking at the poster kind of scares me.

Okay, the real truth is that when I look at the poster, I kind of want to cry or scream or both. I think it's going to give me bad dreams. But I know they meant well, so I hang it on the wall in my room. As soon as they go home, I'm going to take it down off the wall. And I'll put it back up when they come over so they don't think I don't like it, which I do, while at the same time I don't. When I move around the room, I can feel the cougar's big yellow eyes looking at me and it totally freaks me out. Oh well.

In other news, as a surprise, my mum and dad got me a present, too. What is up with all the presents? Do I have to start doling out half-birthday gifts, too? I mean, if you think about it, it's all pretty strange. Not that I don't have a strange family anyway, but this is particularly odd. Anyway, their thing isn't a present at all, actually. It's a thing to do. I hate it when adults call things "presents" which aren't actual things. But anyway, the deal is that I have to take two weeks off diving because my head is all bashed in and stuff and I can't get the stitches wet with chlorine or they might get infected. And then who knows what might happen? I could get blood poisoning and die, which wouldn't be worth it. But for the two weeks that I can't dive, I get to go somewhere else. That's my present.

I get to go to Riding Camp with Montana! Well, I guess it's a good news/bad news story. The bad news is that with my ankle puffed up like a blowfish, I'm not sure I can actually ride (but I'm sure going to try).

The good news is that it's an actual camp. With overnights and everything. Hopefully not with the dumb classes where you make a wallet or whatever, but still.

It's like a real western ranch kind of place and we learn to ride horses and jump them over jumps and stuff. It looks really nice in the brochure. And the really good part of it is that not only will I be away for two weeks, but it means that I can miss Math for Rejects for two weeks! This was not easy. Believe me. Mum was all panicking that I'd fail and not be able to go into Grade Six and then Dad told her that I was going to pass, that I was really just doing this to "help" me with next year's math. That made me furious, to tell you the truth. I thought I was flunking out! I thought it was a matter of life or death! I didn't know it was like an *option*. That's crazy. If I'd known I had a choice, believe me, I would have made a different choice.

Anyway, I've been given all the work to do and Montana (who is obviously a math genius, and an everything-else genius also) will help me with it when we aren't riding horses or otherwise doing fun things. Then I have to take a test that Mr. Whatsit will supervise to make sure I've finally figured out how to multiply fractions or whatever, and then I'm free! Free!

No Nigel for two weeks!

Although now that I know he's not the Porpoise Shooter, I don't hate him as much. This does not mean I like him in any way at all, because I don't.

I will really miss diving, but I've always wanted to learn how to ride a horse. I like horses. I have wanted to learn to ride a horse for my whole life. Horses are like, well, I know this will sound dumb, but they are like land porpoises. Sort of. I mean, they seem really smart. And they have big kind eyes. I wish I had a horse at the cabin because if I was riding a horse and saw a cougar, I wouldn't be scared. The horse would be that much bigger than the cougar and the cougar would run away.

I'm lying on my bed in my quiet new room reading the brochure for riding camp for the billionth time when the phone rings and it's Montana.

"I'm so excited about camp!" I tell her.

"You'll love it," she says. She's been taking riding classes for a little while so she'll be better at it than me, but I don't mind that so much. I look up at the ceiling, which is all white and clean because it's newly painted. I love the smell of new paint. There are no patterns or anything up there to stare at. On my old ceiling, there were cracks and stains that looked like animals or birthmarks.

"I know," I say.

"But never mind that!" she says. "Did you read the paper today?"

"Honestly," I say. "I'm eleven. Who reads the paper when they are eleven?"

"I do," she says.

"Obviously," I say. I roll my eyes even though she can't see me.

"Did you just roll your eyes?" she says.

"Hey," I say, "do you think we're psychic?"

"I don't know," she says. "Maybe."

I try to think a bunch of psychic thoughts to see if she can hear me.

"Carly!" she says impatiently.

"What?" I say. I trace a pattern in the dust on my headboard. It's weird how dusty this room got so quickly. I mean, it's mostly a new room.

"In the paper there was a picture of Nigel's dad and a story about the porpoise shooting!" she says. "They're going to charge the kids who did it with attempted murder of animals — or something like that."

"Can you really do that?" I say.

"Sure," she says. "I guess."

"Were they really kids?" I say.

"Well, no," she says. "I think the article said they were twenty-one."

"Oh," I say. "It's funny how people call twenty-one-year-olds kids."

"Yeah," she agrees.

"Anyway," I say.

"You know," she says. "I was kind of disappointed that Jack Skye's family didn't come to visit us at the cabin."

"Me too," I say, even though I'd forgotten about it until just this moment. "You'd think they'd come by to say thanks."

"I have some news!" she says. "You know how you have to take the ferry to go to the Aquarium? It's the same ferry to get to Riding Camp."

"What?" I say, "I don't understand."

"The Aquarium is in Vancouver," she says slowly, like I'm very very young or stupid or both. "Riding Camp is just outside of Vancouver."

"Is it on the way?" I say, and I can feel myself getting excited.

"Yes!" she says. "It totally is! And Mum says we can take a little detour and visit! Oh, hold on." I hear her mum shouting something from the other room and then there is a clatter when Montana drops the phone on the table. I think it's funny that she does that. I mean, it's a cordless phone so she could have taken it with her but she put it down instead. I think she thinks it has to stay close to the base, which is funny. I mean, it is. But not in a mean way. So I'm laughing a bit when she comes back and says, "Mum says it's actually a really big detour, but we can do it anyway!"

And then I'm so excited I can't stand it. "Whee!" I say.

"I wonder if he'll recognize us!" she says.

"Sure, he will," I say. "Porpoises are really smart." I close my eyes and I start imagining seeing him again and about how once he's released maybe he'll come back to the cabin and visit us and maybe he'll let us play with him in the bay and maybe even let us ride on his back and stuff.

"Maybe he'll come and visit us at the cabin when he's released!" she says, like she was thinking the exact same thing. I'm telling you, it's a bit scary how we think the same way. "That is," she adds, "if I get to go again."

And I can tell she's fishing for an invitation. For a second I feel like telling her that I'm scared to go to the cabin again. The cougar on the wall, which I decided to leave up anyway, looks at me with his yellow eyes. I stick out my tongue at him.

"Of course we will!" I say, more bravely than I feel. "We will," I say again. I think being brave is just like anything else. If you pretend to feel brave, eventually you will feel brave. I wiggle my ankle around and hold it up to look at. It kind of turned black and blue, but it doesn't hurt that much.

"I have to go," she says.

"Me too," I say, and I hobble off my bed and go upstairs to see if Nicholas Zane is awake and baahing. He's getting really cute, I don't mind telling you. He changes so much every day, it's eerie. I thought babies were just babies, but they aren't. They grow like a mile a minute. I guess he's going to change a lot while I'm at riding camp and visiting Jack Skye. I wonder if he'll miss me.

I get upstairs and I can hear Marly yelling, "Mine!" to Shane, and Blue is outside barking, and Mum is yelling "Don't wake the baby!" And I grin a little bit. Because as crazy as it all is, this is the best place in the world to be. And this is the best summer ever.

In spite of the bee sting.

And the wasp sting.

And the jellyfish stings.

And the cut head. Twice.

And the swollen ankle.

I'm sure the rest of the summer will be the Best Ever because, well, I've used up my quota of injuries, haven't I? I've run out.

"Want a ride to the pool?" Dad says.

"What for?" I say. "I can't dive."

"You can swim," he says. "You just have to keep your face out of the water."

"Right!" I say, because he's right. I go back downstairs to grab my suit. I stuff the picture of the cougar under my bed while I'm down there. I mean, I may be brave, but I'm not all the way there yet. But I'm trying, and that has to count for something, right?